May Crommelin

Dust before the Wind

Vol. II

May Crommelin

Dust before the Wind
Vol. II

ISBN/EAN: 9783337067366

Printed in Europe, USA, Canada, Australia, Japan

Cover: Foto ©Andreas Hilbeck / pixelio.de

More available books at **www.hansebooks.com**

DUST
BEFORE
THE
WIND

A Novel

By

MAY CROMMELIN

In Two Volumes

Volume 2

LONDON:

BLISS, SANDS & FOSTER,

CRAVEN STREET, STRAND.

1894.

DUST BEFORE THE WIND.

PART II.—*continued*.

CHAPTER IV.

" . . . alone I carried on and set
My child-heart 'gainst the thorny underwood,
To reach the grassy shelter of the trees.
Ah! babe i' the wood."

WHEN their elders left the tent, Pansy raised herself, while the sparkle of youth came back to her eyes and a faint sweet redness to her lips.

" You *might* have told me!" was all she said, looking with rather severe reproach at Rose.

" What ? I did tell you," replied her sister, in confusion, reddening, conscious of deserving blame.

" You never said he had paid you so much

attention. Now tell me exactly what this wonderful Frank is like," pursued Pansy, inexorably. "How tired we both used to get of hearing his mother talk of, 'my son Frank,' while he was away!"

"Call him 'Mr. Vyner,' dearest. It sounds so very familiar to say 'Frank' behind his back," begged Rose, with the deprecating smile she always assumed when correcting any of Pansy's wayward whims. "And you want to know what he is like? Oh, he has brown hair and a short reddish moustache. His eyes are good—bright blue, with a merry honest look. That's all. What height? Well, middle height; just about a right size, in fact; and then he has such a cheery manner."

"*I* know. He is an ordinary nice fellow, but I should not admire him myself," scoffed the cynical critic. "I prefer dark men."

"As if you had ever seen any worth talking about!"

Rose smiled with supposed superiority, and looked away as far as one narrow vista between the trees permitted; relieved her examination was over.

Ah! Pansy little knew. *He* might be an everyday hero, still that cheerful presence was the central figure of Rose's small world—since seven days ago.

After a schoolroom life of such seclusion that Willow Lea was sometimes nicknamed "The Nunnery" in the village, she had stepped tremulously out into neighbouring society only one brief week back, under Mary Dawson's wing.

And that white day, at her very first party, Rose met Frank Vyner.

Close in Rose's fresh heart lay warm joyous memories of each pleasant word spoken by the young man, of his eagerness to attend to her least wants at tea or at tennis, of his daring request to be allowed to call at the cottage.

Rose could hardly believe her surprised but delighted ears on hearing auntie's gracious consent, coupled with an invitation to come and see Mrs. Dean when the latter should be at home.

Breaking away from these happy thoughts with a conscious start, lest she had betrayed what was, after all, hardly a secret, yet at which that child Pansy would be sure to laugh with sweet mercilessness, Rose looked guiltily round.

Pansy was bending forward, her long lithe arms clasped round her knees, her eyes brimming with mysterious laughter, and a roguish dimple in her left cheek.

"*What is it?* But first, do lie back and rest! How frightfully careless you are, Pansy! There! Now tell me at once. You are hiding some secret."

"Well, if you want to know, I have had an adventure." This given in very, very slow accents.

Then urged, entreated, and coaxed all in turn by Rose, who was fired with curiosity, her young sister unfolded exultingly the story of yesterday's handsome stranger who had rescued kitty from Ophelia's fate.

"But why did you keep it from me all this time?" exclaimed Rose, amazed.

"Because you and auntie were so taken up with your own gay doings at the rectory," retorted Pansy, with fine carelessness cloaking her late secret mortification at having been left at home. "I did begin last night; but neither of you cared to listen. Oh, never mind"—magnanimously, in answer to hasty apologies—"it was very amusing to enjoy it all to myself. If one does tell anything, I find it never seems like one's very own afterwards."

"But you will tell auntie? You know she and mother like to know everything that happens to us," admonished Rose.

"Of course," assented Pansy, with perfect willingness. "It will be such fun to watch her horror. Now, *what* harm can there be in happening to meet a gentleman? Other girls do."

"Mother does not like it."

"Mammie is very prejudiced in some things," returned Pansy.

The remark fell as gently from her lips as some white petals dropped from a haw-thorn tree close by. Then she lay back on her cushions, feeling exhausted, and looking so pale and fragile, that Rose suffered pangs of remorse. She had been too anxious to practise her tennis in order to surprise Mr.

Vyner. Pansy had guessed as much, and so overtasked her own feeble strength, the child's utter unselfishness being a proverb in the cottage.

Mary Dawson had some difficulty that evening in suppressing outward and visible signs of her inward disturbance of mind on hearing Pansy's tale told with artless delight.

"And you talked to this stranger for half an hour, you say? My dear child!" she remonstrated, actually putting down her work a whole half-minute on her lap.

"Of course I did. It was very little to do by way of thanks. Why, except for him, kitty would have been drowned," returned the young culprit, indignantly.

"Who is he? I have not heard of any strange gentleman staying in the neighbourhood," asked the watchful guardian, suspiciously. "You are sure he *was* one, dear?"

"Of course I am," returned Pansy, flushing. Then, in a slightly defiant voice, "He told me he was on a visit at some distance, and had taken a long walk, further than he intended. He said he was going away immediately."

This was the truth. Yet it was not the whole truth.

Even to her sister, Pansy had not confided the stranger's last request to meet him again to-morrow.

Why not?

Well, she had asked herself already that question with an indecision of mind quite unlike her usual swift impulsiveness. Then she vaguely decided to be guided by circumstances.

Mammie and Aunt Mary brought herself and her sister up under too strict surveillance. Oh, she did not rebel, only she lately heard, having the finest of hearing, Mrs. Vyner say so, disapprovingly, to the doctor's wife; and the latter quite agreed, adding that girls were none the worse for a little freedom, and, however well meant, it was hard on young things to be kept in so closely.

Pansy likewise judicially decided in her own mind these on-lookers were right. She knew her own cleverness, and that auntie and Rose always gave in to her opinion as being quicker and clearer than their own. Even her mother, the one being whose superiority the child owned with the most ardent admiration, would nearly always smile excusingly on the rebel's small occasional outbursts of pleading contradiction.

Mrs. Dean had insisted that Mary Dawson must not train her pupils like fruit espaliers, but teach them to think for themselves. She once said that Pansy's clearness of perception especially ought to show her the littleness of much the foolish world deemed important.

This Pansy drank in with both ears, holding her pretty head the higher in consequence.

Now, feeling some dudgeon, she rapidly resolved to say nothing more concerning the stranger.

"How can it hurt me, even if I do meet him to-morrow?" she asked herself with pure maidenly scorn, while a sense of injustice roused youth's quick indignation and sent it thrilling in her veins. "He is a gentleman, and fit to be my friend. After all, I am not so much younger than Rose, and now she is allowed to go to parties to meet people. Perhaps I shall not row that way, after all. Even if I do, I may not happen to see him."

CHAPTER V.

"When violets came, and woods were green,
    And larks did skywards dart,
A love alit, and white did sit
    Like an angel on his heart."

As has been said, Pansy thought awhile, and then hesitated. Should she give up the river this fine day, or not?

A west breeze was blowing, the sunlight glancing through waving green boughs and over rippling grass. Nature itself seemed to be seconding the invitation.

Yet, after all, Pansy might not have gone— not this afternoon. She might not, but for— shall we say?—chance. She called it so herself, but possibly to the unseen cloud of witnesses about us (according to Hebrews), there is no such thing as chance, though perhaps fate, slowly, inevitably shaped long years before by the acts of others, by climate, the play of elements, lastly, our own struggles to gain or escape the likely goal. Instead of chance there may be fightings of the invisible powers of the air, suggested temptations, whisperings of better thoughts, as likewise the workings of nature's laws of heredity within us. Vice is often inborn, transmitted from some self-indulgent ancestor. Unconscious strength to resist evil, to do good, like health of body, may be a gift from another. Oh, we kick against the pricks, but they are in us, in our blood and brain-atoms. Yet still always the one spark is pure, the divine essence, alike in the high-bred of mind as in the human cur. Poor mongrel! feeling stupidly how much easier it is for others to be good. Courage! man is not thy Master; do thy best.

Pansy was as easily blown this way and that as thistledown. One could always reckon on her saying " Yes," even to her own hindrance, to please others; but never with certainty on her keeping to any " No. "

Only yesterday evening Mary Dawson proposed a long walk to-day in search of some especial fern that she and Rose, both ardent botanists, hankered after.

"Then I shall *not* go on the river," decided Pansy, inwardly, with a slight sense of relief that her mind was thus made up for her. She was sorry to disappoint her new friend, but it was impossible to refuse a wish of auntie's.

However, with morning there arrived a note from the doctor's wife, begging Miss Dawson to come to an afternoon party that day, and to bring Rose.

" Mr. Vyner has promised to join us, and we want to make up a set for tennis." So the missive ended.

Rose instantly looked so bright that Mary accepted, though pitying Pansy's loneliness.

" But I never am lonely. I do not know how it feels," replied Pansy with gentle indifference.

This, indeed, was true. The others knew that for half an hour this happy young soul would sit dreaming on a bank of primroses, or idly watching a field of springing wheat stirred by the wind. She could not have told others of her thoughts, but she lived in day-dreams, beautiful, changing. A dangerous habit; for at times her mind was so filled with these rosy mists of fancy that it was difficult to remember she was really only Pansy Dean, of Willow Lea Cottage.

So they left her.

Pansy watched them from the gate, waving her hand after them lightsomely, innocent in face as in heart; yet there was a wistful look in her limpid eyes where an imp called Mischief lay lurking, though a virtuous resolve to be very good weighted the corners of her sweet-lipped mouth.

"I will garden all afternoon," she decided, with a valiant attempt at unpleasing self-denial.

But on looking out her spade and rake in the tool-house, the gardener chanced to pass by.

"What might ye be goin' to dig, miss? Them beds? Lor' sakes! There be bulbs in them. And there's no dead flowers to be snipping at, neither. Now, missy, the plants is best left alone." George, rough priest of Flora, was churlish about *his* plants being meddled with.

Thus repulsed, Pansy wandered off, feeling as

if nobody in particular wanted her. Then—
only too soon—imagination called up a dark,
handsome face looking down the river from
among green boughs—the face of one who was
waiting, watching, perhaps, for her at that very
minute.

If *he* really meant that he hoped to see her
once again, it would be unkind not to go. Oh,
only to give a nod and a smile, and kitty's best
thanks, then drift back down the stream—
nothing more. If he should not be there at all !
Well, who cared ? It was a pleasant day.

Presently a small boat glided out from the
laurel-shaded boat-house by the river's edge.
Slowly Pansy pulled up stream, for the current
was still strong, and her arms never were so,
but she had the practised knowledge of any
waterman. Every twist and turn of the river's
flow thereabouts was familiar to her.

Stroke after stroke she floated on by pastures
where the cows stared down at her from the
low banks like groups by Cuyp, outlined
against the sky. And soon came the ferry with
its sandy road on either side leading down to
the water, hollowed through centuries between

ancient banks, and bordered by giant elms;
then on and on, gliding past a quarry and hanging woods. At last came a still backwater,
where, midway betwixt the brown shining
water and a flowering thicket of thorn and
bramble, an oak tree stood, massive as to girth,
widespread of branches, but comparatively low
in height, truly English in its growth. An
oak is somewhat a type of English architecture
—it grips the soil, it spreads and shelters
widely, but does not soar. The leaf-buds on
the outermost twigs of this monarch oak were
of a tender bronze green, for they were still un-
bursting. Below his branches the turf was so
new-sprung, "shorte and swote," and powdered
with daisies, that Dan Chaucer himself might
have knelt there in glad worship of the May.

And here, only three paces from the bank,
a man stood waiting with folded arms, watching
the point where Father Thames parted his flow
to enfold an islet.

He was the stranger.

Pansy rowed a few strokes irresolutely, then
her boat drifted towards the bank. She glanced
up from under her straw hat, her hands down-

dropped on the oars. Upon all the river, for miles up and down, she was the slightest, most frail-seeming oarswoman to be seen.

The nameless watcher, looking at that ethereal form, with its fugitive, lightly outlined beauty, felt a sudden wish to take up this tender creature in his arms, and carry her through all the rough places of the world. Yet he had thought—long thought—his heart too dead for any such fancies. Quickly stepping down to where the water lipped the overhanging grasses, he greeted his young water-nymph with the same deferential homage of manner that had gratified her childish pride at their first meeting.

What a handsome man he was! Not tall, but so well-proportioned that the least difference would have appeared to mar his almost perfect symmetry. Pansy noticed his eyes flash with pleasure while he was even still at some little distance ; and those wonderful dark hazel eyes now seemed to magnetize her own, so that she looked up at him—and then could not but go on looking.

"How glad I am to see you again!" he

exclaimed. "It was a happy chance for me that you thought of coming out in your boat to-day. Will you not stay and talk for a few minutes, now that luck has already favoured me so much?"

Silly little Pansy! She was greatly relieved that he seemed to think her coming a mere accident; nevertheless, he must have walked far on the chance, if such it was, of seeing her.

"You look like Undine, ready to melt into your native stream," he went on, smiling, as he took hold of her boat. "Now, do pray come up here and rest. Those little hands do not seem strong enough to handle any oars, even such light ones as yours."

"I don't think I will get out, thank you," answered the water-nixie, shyly, yet striving to talk as if quite self-possessed. "And really, I have far more endurance than most people think. For a short distance I can even beat my sister, who rows better than most girls. Rose laughs and says she would make three of me, she is so much bigger and stronger. It half kills me at the time, but if I set myself to do a thing, I generally can."

"Pure spirit! But pluck is not muscle," observed the man.

He was noticing Pansy's arms, bare to the elbow, for she had rolled up the sleeves of her boating jersey. How thin they were!—long, soft, snowy sticks of arms, unformed as yet; but her hands were lovely as those in Lely's pictures, white as milk, rosy-nailed, with long fingers parting slightly as if the better to display themselves, and tapering to delicate tips.

A little while they thus talked. The stranger in his rarely pleasant voice was asking after the kitten, speaking of the beauty of the scene around, the spring greenwood, the sunlight and glancing water; and Pansy murmured back ever more reassured replies. Smiles were beginning to make two fascinating dimples in her young cheeks, and fun was timidly peeping again through her long eyelashes, scared away of late for a while by the great daring of this adventure.

Then said the tempter, bending forward with an air of interest and slight mystery—

"There is something I should like to show you quite near. I have found such a treasure

of a wren's nest. I was waiting here nearly
an hour, and was so still that the birds forgot
to be afraid of me. Then I saw a wren hopping
up to the mossy stump of a tree and disap-
pearing inside it. When he came out again,
I searched there, but could hardly find the
little hole into his green cavern."

Pansy sprang up impulsively, and threw him
the boat's painter.

"Oh, I must see it!"

He fastened the boat securely to a sapling,
and led the way for a few yards, while Pansy
cautiously followed on tiptoe, full of keenest
interest, for she loved bird's-nesting, but would
not have disturbed the feathered parents for
worlds. Being guided to a cushion of deer's-
horn moss, half hidden in grass, she there
dropped on her knees in genuine excitement,
and bent her ear down to a neatly rounded
orifice.

"There are young ones inside," she whispered, delighted; "I can hear them chirping,
'Tweet! tweet! tweet!' What a darling little
home it is for them!"

Pansy was such a child, she was now utterly

happy. Her late scruples, maidenly reserve, all were forgotten, just as if her hair were falling unbound down her back, and she herself still driving a hoop or playing with a skipping-rope.

Not far off lay a fallen log screened by milk-white hawthorns from the fresh breeze, and here her new friend, pleading fatigue after his walk, asked leave to sit down for just a few minutes. Always willing to meet others' wishes, Pansy perched herself on this rustic throne beside him in perfect simplicity, her occasional fits of coquetry blown away like passing clouds, without any other thought in her mind than regret that this pleasant comrade should be tired for her sake.

CHAPTER VI.

" Here is man, indeed,
Not fool or boy : . . .
How fairer is this warrior-face and eyes,
With the sunlight of battle in them left,
As the after-fire of sunset left in heaven,
When the sun sinks, than any fool's face made
Of smiles and courtly colour ! "

How long did these two, who kept tryst for the
first time, stay on their log-seat by the river ?

Pansy did not know.   The moments flew.

And yet it seemed afterwards as if she had
sat there a lifetime, wholly entranced, listening
to the rich voice of the unknown. So a peasant
girl of Provence, in the Middle Ages, might
have hearkened spellbound to the tales of some
troubadour who, passing by her solitary hut,
paused awhile to rest.

He told her of how he had lately returned
from a yachting cruise in the sunny Greek

Archipelago, where the islands lie like jewels set in the glorious "wine-coloured" sea. And because his young hearer was so guileless he became natural too; so spoke of himself, vaguely, it is true, being a man of the world, but with increasing pleasure, as he saw her undisguised interest. He talked of a soldier's life in distant lands; of long marches, thirst, heat, the roar of cannon, dropping rifle fire, cavalry dashes; of the heroic unrewarded deeds of battlefields; of the night silence that fell over an Indian hill fort but lately cleared of border rebels; of the siege of Paris.

It was like listening to a living fairy-tale, a stirring ballad, or modern saga (novels being forbidden fruit, and schoolroom good-goody stories scorned by this fine young intellect, which greatly preferred Shakespeare). Pansy's sensitive being thrilled at these tales of daring, the while she listened with parted lips and eyes eager to outstrip her ears.

"Was there ever such a delightful listener?" he asked himself, in secret enjoyment. It was pure pleasure thus to please this child. Yes, what harm could there be in it?

At last, as he paused, Pansy clasped her hands softly to give herself courage for a great question that was hovering on her lips.

"I do not know your name yet," she said, in a burst of impulse. "You are a brave man, because you are a soldier and have been in battle, and you are *good*. I know that, because you are kind to dumb animals. George the gardener, or even our doctor, would have laughed at my kitten the other day. You were in earnest when you saved it. Please, will you tell me who you are?"

Her companion paused perceptibly for a few seconds before replying.

"I am called Craigdarrock," he said, after inward hesitation. Then, smiling at the engaging child's face, its blue eyes darkened with a world of reverence, "But I am neither great nor good, as you fancy, little one. I might have been so once, who knows? but my career, my life, has been spoilt. It is too late now for fame or happiness."

"Are you not happy, then? I *am* so sorry!"

Pansy's changeable face expressed awed sympathy at once. It even quivered, her emotion being as easily stirred as the leaves of an aspen.

Craigdarrock smiled, straightened himself erect, as if defying fate, gave her a quick, flashing glance.

"I can forget my troubles at times," he replied meaningly; "and I thank you now for one really happy hour."

"That is so little a thing," returned his young companion. "All my life is happy. Or, if I sometimes feel just a trifle melancholy, it is rather pleasant to be sorry for one's self."

"Pleasant! Is it so? May you only know such luxury of woe, never its bitterness, bright child! I, alas!"—and Craigdarrock sighed low, unconsciously, but Pansy's quick ears caught the sound—"I have not known for many years what it is to be genuinely glad, not since I was about as old for a boy as you are for a girl. Looking back, it seems such a wasted existence. And now I am growing old."

"You! Oh no—not old!" protested Pansy, shocked.

Craigdarrock, in the prime of his years,

looked indeed so handsome that she spoke out
honestly her girlish mind. He was more
seductive to her in his noonday of man-
hood than any beardless stripling. She thought
of his soldier's career, of the fighting, privations,
dangers, of which he had so lightly spoken
and that he must have shared. And as
Desdemona was beguiled by Othello's story to a
" world of sighs," even likewise was this equally
young and delicate creature stirred.

"Oh, you must have been sadly unfortunate! But I trust you may still have many
happy years. I do hope that, with all my
heart."

And thus speaking Pansy raised eyes so
wistful with pity melting into softness that—
Heaven forgive him!—Craigdarrock doubted
their utter truth, suspected a little shamming.

Oh, no blame to this tender white witch!
She was one of her sex, and such craft was part
of life's game everlastingly played between
men and women. Many a maiden before had
this man been pleased by, sought to please;
had lent his heart to for a few weeks, cynically
knowing the while he would soon have it

back; had perhaps kept hers for years—who knows?

The game was seldom if ever equal. He owned too great experience of how to win women's love. Even among the world-hardened coquettes, often met with in society's primrose path of gay dalliance, he had once or twice aroused such stormy passion that he himself paused, astonished.

As to a young girl like this delicate Pansy, it was simply sweetly ignorant of her to look in his eyes and try to ensnare *him* with the bands of her too-ready pity. Was she such a child as he had fancied? for girls, like peaches, grow on the " sunny side o' the wall " and ripen soonest.

His hand closed lightly on the small one which rested on the log so near him, as he questioned, with answering softness like her own—

" You feel for me, though you have only seen me twice? Yet you will forget me to-morrow, or a week hence. Then once more, truly, I can say to myself, that not one living soul on this earth cares what happens to me."

The young face he looked at flushed, indignant. Pansy drew away her hand and put it up, vainly sheltering her hot cheek.

"I shall care," she said impetuously but under her breath; "I do not forget; never, never! If I have liked any one, even ever so little, I remember them always."

"Then like me a little—pity me a little!" pleaded Craigdarrock. "Even what you call 'ever so little,' liking is a priceless boon to a world-weary wretch. At times I seem dimly to remember that I was once loved, but that must have been long, long ago."

"I will like you—I do like you," Pansy promised, trembling just a little, though she made her voice sound quite strong and clear.

Craigdarrock recognized the ring of truth. It made a chord vibrate within him that had not resounded this many a day. Under the dead ashes on the altar, too often lit in idle flame, the old fire still glowed then—and he was glad. His heart, unheeding years, still yearned for affection, sought its ideal, however often it had turned away before, disappointed because it had not found the one pearl of great price which only would content it. The man had the gift of expressing his thoughts in his features, and so well could the girl read this mute speech that she faltered out—fluttered, frightened, yet carried away irresistibly by the great tide of pity in her heart—

" Still, liking is so little ! One can *always* be liked, if only by a dog, if we caress it. Surely one wants more than that—a friend who will understand and sympathize in everything, small as well as great. Some one, like part of one's self, who will care for you till you are old and grey, and for whom you care as much or more. That is how I and my sister feel for each other. But no doubt you too—you have——"

" No, no !" he interrupted. " At times I seem dimly to remember that in past years I have been loved—for a while. No one loves me now."

He was very near Pansy. Those dark hazel eyes were bent upon her steadily, and some magnetism seemed to pass from them into the delicate, feminine personality that slightly shrank, yet insensibly gave itself up to the hitherto unknown influence.

Without knowing it, Craigdarrock was wishing his utmost—wishing with all his will, that thoughts of himself should be impressed upon this dear child's tender soul and sensitive virgin heart.

An electric current softly thrilled through the girl's young being. It seemed as if the pity filling her gentle heart was warmed, vivified. A flush of blood rose within her—up, up, from heart to brain. Slowly over her speaking face there dawned a rosy, spreading light. It might be likened to the sun's first rays tinging warmly a snow peak. The man saw, and exulted for a moment that he had the power to rouse this being to such new beauty. And yet he did not wholly understand, though perhaps a little in part.

Craigdarrock caught Pansy's two snow-flakes of hands in his own strong, warm ones, on an impulse answering her emotion. Pansy did not dare to look up. She drooped, so troubled by the new-born spirit within her, that, like Horace's young Chloe, shy as a fawn scared by

the breeze in the forest and the spring shudder-
ing through green leaflets, she was seized with
a panic, her heart and her knees were a-tremble.
Then her hands slipped softly out of his grasp,
as if he had been holding a spirit-creature, an
elusive creation in the image of woman. Turning away, she took a long bough of white-
flowered wild cherry, and bent her face down as
if to inhale its delicate fragrance; but under
her wide straw hat he could just see that her
under-lip trembled finely.

"I must go. I must leave you now," she
murmured. "And you—you are not coming
back to these parts, you say?"

"There is but small chance of my doing so, I
fear."

"Good-bye. I am sorry."

Craigdarrock hesitated within himself, looked
hard at her averted head. Thoughts she could
not guess at were holding a skirmish within
him. Forces were being arrayed for and
against—for good or evil. Only a skirmish
now; in the days to come it might be a battle.
Bah! too soon to reckon with the future.

And how graceful this slender white figure

was, with its pre-Raphaelite background of
bare cherry twigs outlined against the blue sky
overhead, while lower down the thicket was
dotted with a green shower of unfolding hazel
buds! Then her eyes. Among hundreds of
women he had never seen such eyes as hers,
like beautiful gentians. She was a blue-eyed
gazelle.

Stifling inner warnings, Craigdarrock hastily
muttered—

"There might be just the ghost of a chance."
He said it as if arguing with himself, and went
on musingly, "Not for some weeks, anyhow.
But then, say in June, or even towards the end
of May, I *might* manage it."

Pansy had turned her face towards him like
a marigold (the true sunflower) to the sun,
reassured by the tone of the speaker's voice that
he was not actually addressing herself.

Smiling at the sweet visage that was verily
no less delicate than the petals of a briar rose,
Craigdarrock continued, gaily and directly—

"Yes! If you cared to see me, dear little
friend of two blissful hours—if you really cared,
say, half as much as you did to have your kitten

back again, why then—who knows? Difficulties might vanish ; distance, time seem mere trifles. One might even venture a promise to put a girdle round the earth in forty minutes."

"Of course I must care. Are we not friends, as you said just now?" murmured Pansy, reproachfully, while her fingers nervously broke off a spray of cherry blossom. "Do I see so many people at Willow Lea that I should forget? You *know* you are the only stranger——"

She broke off abruptly, for on their previous meeting Craigdarrock had learned from her artless talk all there was to tell of Pansy's brief history till then.

A convent-bred girl would have had far more knowledge of human nature, of the great world outside, learnt from the little world of schoolfellows and teachers. Three human beings had hitherto peopled Pansy's circle—mother, auntie, and Rose. For other interests she sought her pets and birds ; fields, woods, flowers, pages of the great green book she loved to ponder from babyhood. So he could guess what a stirring, romantic experience this sudden friendship with himself must seem in her fresh eyes, which

looked at him much as do those of a baby at
some new object displayed to its gaze.

"You remind me of the Lady of Shalot,"
said Craigdarrock, caressing admiration taking
possession of his eyes, his voice sounding delightful in Pansy's ears as strange music.
"Like you, the Lady of Shalot grew up lonely
by the river, and only saw shepherd lads and
lasses and Lancelot go by in her magic mirror.
So you read in books of men and women, young
men and maidens, who live and love outside
your hidden cottage."

Unwittingly he had stumbled on the simile.
The moment after the words left his lips, it
flashed across them both that if she was the
Lady of Shalot, who then was Lancelot? And
each knew what the other was thinking:
thought is communicated so strangely at
moments from mind to mind when these are
attuned to each other.

Giving an embarrassed laugh, Craigdarrock
went on almost abruptly—

"Well, if I do come, how shall I let you know
that your new friend is in the neighbourhood?
Shall I adventure myself through your lodge

gate and up to the door, like the Prince breaking through the wood round the Sleeping Beauty's castle ? "

" Oh no, no! Please do not, because, you see, I am not considered grown-up yet," objected Pansy, earnestly. " Isn't it ridiculous ? Rose is so little older, and she was ' brought out ' last week at a party. Frank Vyner is to be allowed to visit us now. You do not know who he is ;—our rector's son just come back from Australia. He is the only young man in our neighbourhood. My sister met him out at her first tennis-party, and mother has allowed him to call to-morrow; then I shall see him."

" Ah ! he has not seen *you* yet."

The faintest idea of a possible rival in the future acted like a spur upon Craigdarrock's lingering resolve. His mind was made up on the instant.

" When I come back, will you look out for me by the paddock gate, then, near the wood ? " he suddenly said in a half-whisper, though only a white butterfly zigzagging in the air could have overheard the tryst.

"Yes. I will go every day—that is, if you really mean it," murmured Pansy.

"If I do not find you when I return, I shall leave a sign," went on Craigdarrock, bending his head, noting with secret pleasure the breathlessness of shy joy with which she welcomed the hope of seeing him again. "Shall I carve a 'C' upon the gate-post? No, no, that would not do. Stay, are there not willows close by? I shall always think of you when I see a willow, so if you find a branch fastened into the hasp, you will know I have come—that you will see me soon."

Lingeringly they parted. The little boat slowly drifted down stream. Pansy hardly moved the oars as yet, she only held a straight course, and kept looking at Craigdarrock as long as she could see him. He had taken off his hat and held it raised in farewell while he too watched her with answering smiles, till both faces grew indistinct and the smiles were imagined, and the dinghy drifted round a curve and was lost to sight.

"She is exquisite!" he soliloquized aloud, yet under his breath. "I ought not to come back."

Then he laughed harshly, and a stern look came into his eyes.

" *Ought not?* What of that? I must see that wonderful light making an aurora over her face once more. I must kiss her lips, those soft, fresh lips, some day. No man, I will swear, has ever kissed them yet."

CHAPTER VII.

"I did but look and love a-while,
    'Twas but for one half-hour;
Then to resist I had no will,
    And now I have no power."

THE rain was falling next day.

A fly drove up in the afternoon to the
Willow Lea gate, where a lady dressed in black
stepped out of the vehicle. She was a tall,
elegant woman.

Three figures inside the drive were waiting,
huddled together under the shelter of a giant
yew-tree and of their umbrellas. These were
Mary Dawson and her two pupils.

"Darling mother!" cried Rose and Pansy,
springing forward to greet the new-comer with
embraces and caresses.

Each caught their mother by one arm, while
their umbrellas knocked overhead, vying which
should protect her.

"There, there! Spare me till we are under shelter," Stella laughingly cried. "I have as many rain-drops as kisses on my face. Come, you are ducks, both of you, I grant that, but I am not so fond of water. I am a barn-door hen clucking over her chicks."

"You are a swan," put in Pansy—"a black swan." She had gained the day in the battle of umbrellas, and was dragging her willing captive up the slushy gravel.

"You are a goose, Pansy," added Rose—"a gosling, a green gosling. My umbrella is biggest, and mammie will get wet."

Meanwhile Mary Dawson had paid and dismissed the flyman.

The mistress of Willow Lea never allowed a carriage to pass her wooden gate and go up the few yards of drive to the cottage. It was one of her whims. Wheels cut up the gravel, she curtly said if questioned; and where was the good of encouraging the young maids to stand gossiping with strange men?

The said maids pouted their rosy faces a little. They came from a distance, and were never required to stay longer than nine months.

In the height of summer-time Willow Lea was
let to strangers, just when the season was at
its flush, and there were the excitements of big
houseboats moored close by with gay parties
on board, and smaller craft continually passing
up and down from Oxford ; when artists or
other happy-minded bohemians were camping
out in the meadows, and every spare room in
the village was let to jaded Londoners pining
for fresh air. Only one old servant always
remained. She had been nurse to the two girls.

With the weekly arrival of the mistress, a
little breeze of excitement used to ripple the
usual still surface of existence in the cottage.
Maids were busied two days beforehand polish-
ing mirrors and brasses, dusting every article
of furniture to spotless perfection. The girls'
chatter and laughter, as Stella declared, reminded one of a whole flock of young sparrows
asking each other about the day's events at
roosting-time.

Presently there was a bright scene in the
drawing-room, where Mary, as housekeeper,
was dispensing tea from behind a little table
loaded with glittering silver and delicate china.

Stella herself was lying back in a deep arm-chair resting after her journey, while on a foot-stool at her side Pansy had crouched down, like a happy child, resting against her mother's knees and caressing her hand with loving touches.

Rose, good Rose, felt a little enviously that she would have liked to do the same; but then her duty was to bring her mother's teacup and minister to her creature comforts, "to be my Martha," as Stella said, with a consoling, affectionate glance at her fair-haired daughter. She read Rose like an open book. She understood quite well that the elder girl yearned to see her back each week, just as wistfully as the young creature at her feet, in whose life Stella's own seemed bound up. And she loved her eldest daughter truly too, but Pansy was her darling, her heart's very core. She was sorry to be partial, but she could not help it.

Presently there came a ring at the door that pealed with unaccustomed vigour through the little house. It "fluttered the dovecote." The thought flashed through Stella's mind, followed by an inward, half-satirical laugh.

Rose stood arrested, a teacup in her hand. A

glad surprise brightened her face into almost
beauty.

" Oh, it must be——" she ejaculated.

" Mr. Frank Vyner," explained Mary, from
behind the tea-urn.

" Coriolanus," added Stella aloud, ending her
previous thought, which her listeners did not
grasp.

It was Frank Vyner truly enough. He had
received a slight invitation to call that day to
make Mrs. Dean's acquaintance, and, undeterred
by the rain that had kept persistently falling
since morning, here he was.

" Frank by name and nature," was Stella's
keen criticism. She liked his open brow, ruddy
cheek, and the ready smile which both lit up
his eyes and disclosed two rows of even white
teeth, as, on coming in, his seeking glance perceived Rose's expectant figure.

" We hardly thought you would come on
so bad a day," murmured the girl, shyly, as she
introduced him to her mother.

" Oh, why not ? A little wetting does not
hurt me," returned Frank, with a good-
humoured laugh, looking somewhat astonished

at this mother of whom he had heard so much. Somehow he had never imagined her so young looking and—so handsome. Fresh from a lonely station life, he little guessed that artificial means could preserve or copy original beauty so wonderfully well.

Stella's figure was still unusually slight. Under her travelling hat and veil her complexion seemed almost as fresh as that of a girl, her dark hair as abundant.

"Ah! you have come from Australia lately, Mr. Vyner, they tell me," said his hostess, in a cordial voice that relieved honest Frank of embarrassment as by magic. It was a voice, he said afterwards, that made him feel somehow as if he had been friends with her all his life. "You have not got the affected, effeminate ways of so many of our town-bred, gilded youths. It quite does one good to meet a man who is superior to weather and will consent to make the best of our island climate."

A merry answer was rising to Frank Vyner's lips, when at that very moment he almost started and looked as if magnetized. By what——?

Stella sharply turned her head and saw that
he was staring transfixed at Pansy, who was
still crouched on her velvet cushion, and who
till that instant had been hidden by her mother
from his observation. She also was looking at
him. Just one large, inquiring glance out of
her radiant eyes, as might a fawn couched in
the covert. No more.

Stella pleasantly motioned to the visitor to
sit down near the tea-table between herself and
Rose. She then laughingly introduced Pansy
with a slight wave of her hand as, "my second
daughter, my little schoolroom girl."

Talk flowed as lightly and cheerily as the tea-
urn sang over its spirit flame. Somehow in
Stella's company those she liked felt inspirited
to show off at their best, for she had a clever
way of bringing out their strong points. Even
dull folk quite shone to their own surprise,
little guessing they were mere moons, borrow-
ing some passing radiance from her solar heat
of vitality. She herself was brilliant in conver-
sation, and Rose and also Mary Dawson, who
threw in a chirping, bright observation now
and then, with Vyner himself, were all as merry

as could be, sipping their tea and nibbling buttered tea-cakes.

Frank Vyner chatted most with Rose; naturally so, for she knew him best. But, even while questioning and answering, his eyes strayed constantly, try to remember his manners as he might, towards the unconscious young beauty in the background.

When the visitor entered, Pansy had noticed, in a fleet, careless glance, that he wore gaiters buttoned over thick-soled, clumsy boots, fit certainly for tramping in muddy lanes, but not pretty objects in themselves. At another time it would have been exciting to make the acquaintance of a new-comer, but when her darling mother had just arrived home it was rather annoying than otherwise to have their first gush of family confidences and eager questionings thus suddenly interrupted. Then, too, in her own mind Pansy had a new standard of manly excellence by which to judge all other men. In thought she saw constantly a dark, well-shaped head, gleaming eyes that were dark also in shadow, but hazel in the sunlight, a delicate, slightly aquiline nose,

and high-bred features; all these external
qualities being heightened by a distinguished
air, which is in both men and women as the
scent to the flower, and beside which Frank's
rustic, breezy manner seemed almost vulgar.
Besides, *he* had white, well-shaped hands,
although he wore no gloves, and spoke as if
sport, handling a gun, an oar, a salmon-rod,
were his chief delights. And though she
could not have told what Craigdarrock's boots
were like, this critical young creature knew
that they had seemed a fitting part of himself,
therefore akin to perfection. So she put up
her dainty nose and looked airily out of the
window at the thick-dropping rain.

Next she tempted Sprite, her mother's pet
toy terrier, on her own lap by silent wiles.
She hugged and teased it; made it sit up
begging for crumbs.

Vyner was giving a confused, laboured
account just then of his Australian experiences
to Mrs. Dean, while Rose sat by listening to
every word with a deep interest she tried to
conceal by staring at the carpet.

Suddenly the speaker interrupted himself,

burst out laughing, and exclaimed reproachfully to Pansy—

"Poor little beggar, how you are tantalising him!"

Sprite's tormentor started in surprise, not thinking he had observed her by-play.

"Mr. Vyner is right," put in Stella, good-humouredly. "You are a sad child, Pansy, an embodied sprite of mischief yourself. I see you like dogs," she went on, smiling in an open, cordial way upon the young man; "you must see our setter puppies—four black-and-tan Gordon beauties. I dare say you are a judge. You will be able to tell us which promise best. Rose, you are their proud owner; you had better display them, dearest. They are better than babies, inasmuch as they are always ready to be shown off to visitors, and don't cry."

Rose brightly rose at once to seek out her sprawling treasures. These were kept in the unused stable, and as a covered passage led round the tiny cottage yard there was no risk of a further wetting, so good Mary Dawson kindly informed the young man. She had noticed that he seemed to hesitate a moment, and she mistook the cause of his lingering.

" Won't you come, too? " he said, moving towards the door, but then turning and looking back at Pansy.

The invitation was so directly given that the latter rose to her feet, indifferently enough, for though she adored the puppies she would have preferred staying with her mother.

" Yes, of course," nodded Stella, lightly, as if taking the matter for granted.

So the young people went out.

When they were gone, mother and auntie looked across the tea-table significantly and gave each other a small but meaning nod.

They were not smiling.

Before Frank Vyner took his leave he disburthened himself of a particularly pleading message from his mother, that Miss Dawson and Rose should spend another long afternoon at the Rectory next week. Tennis, of course, was the pretext.

(" It used to be croquet when I was a girl," mused Stella, but she did not say so aloud. It was her unconscious habit to say nothing

that reflected on her age, and indeed it was
only at Willow Lea she remembered her own
added years in looking at her tall, slim
daughters; and yet only here at times she felt
something that was akin to happiness.)

Frank was not satisfied with merely the
willing acceptance of his invitation. He himself added a postscript with an eagerness which
betrayed it was by no means unimportant in
his eyes.

"But Miss Pansy will be allowed to come
also, I hope. Would you not like to come?
You play tennis, I am sure." Then without
waiting for any answer he went on eagerly,
turning to Stella, "Mrs. Dean, will you not
allow your youngest daughter to come to us,
too? It is not as if we were strangers, and
we shall be quite by ourselves next Tuesday.
Please do! we shall count upon seeing her,
Miss Dean."

And his white teeth showed in such an
eager smile at Rose, that the latter, who wanted
no urging, at once became a warm ally in his
suit.

"Oh yes, darling, do please say Pansy may

go with us," she pleaded. "I was telling
Mr. Vyner only the other day that I could not
enjoy myself half as much without her, for we
sisters were never separated in anything until
I came out."

"Well, well; we will see when the day
comes," answered Mrs. Dean, evasively but
graciously, with a fascinating smile.

She darted a keen glance towards Pansy,
who alone took no part in the discussion.
She was standing statue-like in the background,
with a dreamy expression in her limpid eyes
and the smile of a young Mnemosyne on her
lips.

It was all alike to her what the others
decided; she would be equally happy now,
whether taken with them or left at home.

CHAPTER VIII.

" Were it not thus, O King of my salvation,
  Many would curse to Thee, and I for one,
Fling Thee Thy bliss and snatch at Thy damnation,
  Scorn and abhor the shining of the sun;
Ring with a reckless shivering of laughter,
  Wroth at the woe which Thou hast seen so long,
Question if any recompense hereafter
  Waits to atone the intolerable wrong."

LATE that night, when the two young sisters were already asleep upstairs in their pretty chintz-hung rooms, one rose-and-white nest, one blue-and-white, adjoining each other, their mother and adopted aunt were still in the drawing-room holding a confidential talk. Though the spring was far advanced, a small wood fire was reflected brightly in the tile-lined grate. Both women had drawn their armchairs near its glow and were evidently prepared " to have a good chat."

" Now to render an account of my stewardship for this last week," Mary Dawson had just said.

Every time when the mistress of the house came home on one of her usual flying visits they held this same midnight consultation. There was but one subject discussed, that which was dearest to the hearts of both—their living treasures, "the children," as mother and foster-mother called the two girls still.

"And so this Vyner lad has been attentive to Rose, you wrote me," began Stella, without any preliminary, a little frown of thought puckering her white brow. "He looked to me as if it would suit very well. Only, this after-noon I was afraid——"

"This afternoon he saw Pansy," brusquely interrupted Mary Dawson. "He was 'struck all of a heap.' I noticed the difference in a moment. How can we expect any man to look even at as nice a girl as Rose, when that young Venus is by? He should not have seen them together."

"He must have seen them both sooner or later," replied Stella, in a disturbed voice, pride in her darling's singular powers of fascination struggling with solicitude and affection for her other daughter. "After all, no harm may be done yet. Does Rose care for him? You must see; you must know. You have eyes."

"But I have no experience," bluntly confessed poor Mary, troubled in her turn. "Rose likes him, of that I am sure. She was greatly pleased by his attentions, but you saw that to-day no thought of jealousy crossed her mind. After all, if it should be Pansy, it may still all be for the best."

"*How could it be?* No, no! It would suit Rose excellently well. From all accounts I have heard of him since he was a lad, Frank Vyner is as good as gold, and he is going back to Australia again. Rose would like the life out there; but as to Pansy! the very thought of parting with her for years would really kill me."

Stella was deeply moved, and spoke with almost indignation in her voice against her companion for suggesting such an idea. Then, the latter being prudently silent, the mother resumed with a sigh—

"I have never foreseen this contingency.

You know I have always intended that Rose should marry first and happily before Pansy could interfere with her prospects. The child ought to make a brilliant match. *You* know— even *you* acknowledge, Mary, that she is a gem, a pearl of rarest price."

"What if both girls should get to care for this lad? He is not bad looking, and there are no other men here."

"God forbid—how cruel that would be of fate! The only thing I still long for on earth, strive for day and night, is to ensure that both my children shall be happy. What harm is there in that? Why should it be denied me, I ask you?"

"Dear, you want to play Providence," returned Mary with outspoken candour. "Can you preserve your darlings against illness, accidents in trains or carriages, by fire or water? You must accustom yourself to the idea that they will most likely suffer now and again like the rest of us; it is the human law."

"I do not mind pain any longer for myself, but I could not bear to see them suffer," said Stella, gloomily. "Oh, what a weary world!

And why was it made so? I could have made
a much better one, I know, with no sins, no
sorrows, no sickness. We two sit here, cosy
and well, and at this very moment how many
wretched beings all over the world are gasping
out their last breath in the agonies of death!
A little while ago, when the lamp was lit and
the window still open, how we were all enjoying
ourselves! and there fluttered in a pretty night-
moth and was burned. Out on the lawn just
now, I dare say a field-mouse is creeping somewhere to its nest, and an owl is sure to swoop
down and pounce upon it; or a rabbit is playing in the moonlight outside its burrow, and
it will be caught by the throat and its blood
sucked out by a stoat. Why should there be
evil or pain—can you tell me that?"

"Oh, why?" retorted Mary, vexed, rousing
herself from her comfortable lounge to sit upright, as if more capable in that position of
grappling with the question. "Am I wiser than
the many millions who have been born, that I
should answer this thing? Only, in the Book of
Genesis, which you consider a hoary legend,
and that I, at least, reverence as a divine alle-

gory, there is a mention, you may remember, of a Power of Darkness, the Prince of this world —the old Devil, in plain English. Well, he is not dead yet; and I firmly believe that all sorrow and pain are his wicked work."

"The old fable of light and darkness, of good and evil," dreamily came from Stella's lips. "It may be as you say. Forgive me if I hurt you, Mary dear, just now. I assure you that I only wish I could believe in a future as you do. But what proofs have we?"—her voice rising crescendo—"what proofs? Has ever any one returned to tell us if there really is a spirit-world?"

"The Jews of old sought a sign, and none was given them," replied Mary, stoutly holding her ground. "There are many things in daily life I feel pretty sure of, although with no good reason to show : call it faith, instinct, intuition, what you like. And I *do* feel sure of living when my body dies. I can imagine myself living hundreds of years hence—with all my memory, my likings and loves for different people, and perhaps any little learning also acquired here on earth. It is rather a good thing that my body will die; a worn-out, wrinkled, aching old husk it will be, if it lasts long enough. I shall feel very glad, I dare say, once I am well out of it and away."

"But still it is strange, you will grant, that no spirits, if there are such, ever have come back," reiterated Stella. "Ghosts do not count, nor apparitions of dying people. I mean, no one has ever returned with a warning from the other side of the grave; and yet how useful —how all-important it might be to us! We should lead very different lives, if we were quite sure of what comes after death."

"So the Jews thought when the parable of Dives and Lazarus was taught to them," as obstinately returned Mary; "and the Teacher I follow declared, if they would not listen to Moses and the Prophets neither would they hear though one spoke to them from the dead. All the same, I firmly believe some have come back. One did, that is, our Blessed Lord; so did Lazarus; and on the Mount both Moses and Elias were seen in a vision——"

"Oh, if you believe all that——!"

"I do. And more—from Genesis on. But

we must read the spirit, not the letter. Still much is pure history."

"But many of the big brains say that Christ was a fanatic—a beautiful character, but a visionary," objected Stella. "Mohammed is also a historical fact; Buddha——"

"Mohammed did not make the world any happier. In fact, he has hindered its growth by preventing the spiritual and mental development of millions of women."

"True. How can mothers who are no better than human sea-anemones bear sons of brain-fibre equal to those whose two parents are intelligent beings?" Stella dryly remarked, as if to herself. "Go on, little Mary. I frankly claim a freedom for women that might shock you, because, not being certain of any future life except a resolving into our original elements, my nature cries out to enjoy this short, conscious existence, as men do. You and I would never agree, but it interests me to see how differently we look at these things. What of Buddha? his doctrine was beautiful, they say."

"Yes, so they say, and I have read beautiful descriptions of his life, but still, I wonder do we

Europeans really know much about his teaching?" said Mary, thoughtfully. "However, if it is so pure, let us accept him gladly as a messenger of good tidings to mankind. Surely also Plato, Cicero, and many more were given their lamps to lighten our darkness. And why may we not look upon Shakespeare, Goethe, Raphael, Michael Angelo, as inspired too, each in his own way—— ?"

"Inspired! You enthusiast!"

"Yes," smiled Mary, with a happy expression. "All given gifts and messages from pleasant courts above. Oh, do not let us, poor worms with little brains, be so perplexed because we cannot understand many things in this life of ours. Does a mole burrowing in his brown earth understand the flight of a bird in the sunshine? The angels desire still to look into some things, we are told; and how much clearer vision and deeper wisdom they must have than mere creatures of dust! A thousand years hence, you and I may discuss all this over again, dear—and smile at it."

"If we meet." The dreary, doubting answer fell slowly from Stella's lips.

There was a silence in the room. Could they
two tell, indeed, if they might ever meet in the
unknown country? Even Mary said nothing
and was perturbed, she knew not exactly why.

Then an agitated whisper came from Stella.

" Oh, Mary, teach my daughters, if you can,
to feel as you do. You believe also there are a
paradise and purgatory, as in the parable, don't
you? not alone heaven and hell-fire for ever.
All I ask is to be annihilated—to pass into
nothingness; to forget! *What is the truth?* "
Her voice broke off in a sharp wail.

" All creeds are like shattered fragments of a
great mirror of Truth, I believe; or the different facets of a diamond," answered Mary,
wiping her eyes furtively, to which tears had
sprung some time before, when her dear friend
and benefactress revealed glimpses of an inner
wretchedness of mind which the little woman
shuddered at without understanding. " It
doesn't exactly matter which part is looked into
so long as you see there that God is good and
is Love. Only, He must suffer our sins to
work their punishment, for our own sakes."

" My hell began some years ago, and has

been burning in me ever since," muttered Stella, with a strange light in her eyes. "I have read something like that in Marlowe's 'Faust' —that 'hell is here,' nor are we out of it. You never cared much for classical reading, Mary. A mistake that. Life has so few real pleasures. Don't mind what I have been saying. We women are so hysterical." And she gave a short, hard laugh.

Neither spoke awhile.

Mary, after the real effort of this fervent and unusually long utterance of the faith that was in her, leant back once more, troubled and tired; her heart no longer hot, its fire died low.

Stella's brows were knitted as she stared at the hearth, now filled with glowing ashes. She was thinking—thinking. Suddenly she began, without preamble, confident of being understood.

"If they marry bad men, our care will all have been wasted; and what care we have both given—you and I! Then, though I know men better than you do, better than most women, our innocents may insist on choosing for themselves.

You believe there is a divine spark in all of us. But I solemnly declare to you, I know men so evil that if it ever was there it must have died out; only their bodies and minds are really living. They themselves say they *know* there is no future for them, and I sometimes imagine they may be right—that they have killed their spirits, which is possibly meant by ' the second death.'

> ' *On entre, on crie,*
> *Et c'est la vie,*
> *On crie, on sort,*
> *Et c'est la mort.'*

Now, all I know is—that *I don't know.*"

Surely, thought her listener, Stella was in a strange mood to-night, flippant and solemn in the same breath. Mary gently protested.

"Perhaps none are so bad as you think. I dare say, even for the worst of these men, that some women would be found to love them and to weep for them, as the slave Acte did for Nero ; and while any one pure, striving soul prays for another, I think that other soul is invisibly strengthened."

"A woman's certain misery with a bad man

might help his possible salvation! It is a risk I prefer not running," Stella sarcastically commented. "Of course, as long as I am alive, I can and will guard my daughters; and though I believe that, as society is at present constituted, a girl's best chance of happiness is to be married, still marriage is a very terrible engagement, and so binding for life—even to drunkards, or madmen, or criminals—that I will take good care only to allow fairly good and eligible men to know them."

"Ah!" put in Mary, anxiously, "I have often wished lately to speak to you on that very point. You have insisted on their being brought up so utterly innocent, even far more so than any other girls I have ever known or heard of; and innocence, when it is also ignorance, has its dangers."

Stella pooh-poohed her friend's anxieties on this score.

"You and I are here to judge for them, to advise them. They take my opinion in everything as gospel."

"But again I say we cannot play Providence," reiterated Mary. "There is this

stranger whom Pansy met the other day. She
has told you about him ? "

" Yes ; she told me he is a Mr. Craigdarrock,
a passing visitor, and that he was to leave the
neighbourhood two days after. Craigdarrock—
I seem to have some vague recollection of the
name ; " and Stella tried to recollect, in vain,
where and when she could have heard it. " I
did not say much to her about him. It would
have made too great a matter of a chance
affair, and the danger is past."

" It is growing late," Mary ventured to
observe, glancing at the clock, being accus-
tomed to early hours herself, " and you have
not yet settled what I am to do about Mr.
Vyner."

" Let him meet Rose as much as possible,"
decided Stella, swiftly. " Keep Pansy out of
his way, only do not let him notice you are
doing so. He is more fitted for Rose. He
must marry her, if either."

" If he marries her, you will have to tell
him her real name," timidly put in the little
family counsellor. " I often wish, Stella dear,
you had not taken back your maiden one ; it

may make such complications. Why, the girls do not even know that their father was Mr. Morice."

"I hate my married name, and I had my own reasons for doing so," answered Stella, unwillingly and curtly. "Of course, when Rose marries I must explain matters, as you say. Time enough then."

"But you are known in London, in your business, are you not, as Mrs. Morice?" blundered on Mary, in a sleepy voice.

"Well, what of that?" demanded Stella, with such a harsh ring in her voice that Mary opened her blinking eyes and sat bolt upright. "I have my own reasons, as I told you before; let that be sufficient between us." Then, in quick contrition, with some tenderness of tone, "There, do not vex me, Mary; you do not often do so, I must say. Come, good night. It is getting late" (it was an hour and more past midnight), "and let us hope that all will go well with our darlings in life."

"You must trust; you must let them be prepared to suffer some burdens, like all other sons and daughters of men," Mary gathered her wandering wits to say. Then she yawned and felt ashamed of herself.

Stella, who seemed to have a constitution of steel, smiled superior to any such weakness as sleepiness, it seemed. So they also went to rest.

CHAPTER IX.

"This day Dame Nature seemed in love;
The lusty sap began to move.

.   .   .   .   .   .

Already were the eaves possessed
With the swift pilgrim's daubèd nest.

.   .   .   .   .   .

The showers were short, the weather mild,
The morning fresh, the evening smiled."

On passed the stately procession of days, flower-scented, shower-laden; some shrewish and chill, blighting the fair promise of fruit; others glad, with the first swallows darting in circles round the grey church tower in the village, dipping their wings in low flight athwart the surface of the ceaselessly flowing river. One afternoon the cuckoo's "wandering voice" was heard on a sudden, for the first time this year, among the trees. On and on the days came, born with the rising sun, dying at eve. "One day telleth another: and one night certifieth another. There is neither speech nor language: but their voices are heard among them."

And what did their passing tell Pansy? Only that each one sped brought her so many hours nearer the goal to which she eagerly, impatiently looked forward; that she rejoiced as every night fell softly over the valley, Father Thames flowing, as for thousands of years, on and on between his sedgy banks and dewy lawns, and on either hand the woods that grew daily a darker green. Her heart whispered so often each day, "*He is coming back*," that never had spring seemed so divine before. Messages of delicious hope were breathed in this young creature's ears by every breeze laden with new fragrance, as lilac-tide waned, but a still braver show of flowers was bursting out everywhere—on the cottage walls, in the garden, and by the river's banks, to the glory of summer.

Often during these days Pansy would suddenly turn aside her head from observation, or find a pretext to hide a smile of inner rapture that would rise unawares and ripple

over the dreamy calm of her face.   And
because love teaches so aptly even the merest
chit of a girl to feign like any practised actress,
so this young deceptress hid her secret well.
No one noticed any change in Pansy except
that she alternated between feverish fits of
devotion to her studies and increased love of
solitude.   It was all to please Craigdarrock;
to dream of him.   Her heart was like an
incense-brazier, burning to the praise of her
demi-god day and night.   She held long hours
of talk with him while her slim figure wandered
up and down her now favourite path by the
willows fringing the weir.   She told him all
her joys and tiniest sorrows, even shy, girlish
fancies, budding ambitions, romantic ideas she
would scarcely have dared unfold to any other
living being.   But *he* understood all !   In rose-
tinted visions she vaguely imagined scenes lived
together in the future, shrinkingly yet rapturously, with such exquisite, delicate pleasure as
no reality could equal.

Again romantic sentiment would picture a
night scene after battle : dews were falling, a
cold moon rising, the howl of a jackal heard

in the distance. Alone, Craigdarrock would
be lying with white, unconscious face upturned
to the star-strewn sky. Then she, passing on
an errand of mercy through the heaps of slain,
and wreck, and carnage of the fight, would
find him—succour, tend him back through sickness to health again, and he would call her his
good angel who brought healing on her wings.

Or again fancy danced more gaily to a tune
of joyous, inspiriting music. They met, he
and she, in gay crowds, where princes and
great painters, peers and poets, a brilliant and
titled throng, surrounded Miss Pansy Dean, the
new star of the season, whose praise was the
theme of every tongue. Turning from them
all, she would gently, smilingly single out
Craigdarrock for some slight yet precious token
of her favour. She would see him standing
somewhat aloof, more distinguished than all
the rest, and he would give her one glance
from a distance that would flash with more
lustre to her mind, far outweigh in value all
the diamond stars and blue ribbons and decora-
tions around her.

Steeped in such visions, this childish dreamer

hardly thought what might happen when Craigdarrock really came back.

When Pansy did return to real life, it was only to promise herself that, for a little while, she would first gloat all alone over the treasure of his friendship—his dear looks, the clasp of his hand, the tones of his low, caressing voice, that crept into and all about her heart like a strain of music that sometimes would move her to a gush of happy tears. Why, his presence already had at moments made her own sense of individuality grow indistinct, so that she only knew *he was there*—nought else mattered.

Then some day, ah! yes, a red-letter day, she would reveal her happy secret. With what surprise, but immediate gladness, her small world of dear ones was sure to regard this man of men! How triumphantly Pansy meant to watch the almost awestruck admiration that would spread over their faces as they came to know her hero! How she already laughed in her heart, but not aloud, feeling truly sorry that Rose had never known so blissful, so delightful an adventure! Then they would praise him to her, aside, with

generous envy, and even mother — darling
mother—whose opinion her daughters almost
dreaded in its severity of criticism upon all
matters of good taste (for Stella was to them
a final tribunal of appeal), even she would say
that she had never seen a more gallant and
handsome soldier, or so distinguished and perfect a gentleman. Thus the flame of love leapt
higher and higher, fed on fancy, in this yet
childish heart.

Mrs. Dean, as she called herself, did not
return to Willow Lea for a fortnight after her
last visit. The little household met her with
affectionate scoldings, redoubled embraces, reproachful accounts of their lamentations at her
absence.

"Ah! nothing like staying away to make
one properly valued," Stella laughingly replied, evading promises for the future, parrying
inquiries.

"Business kept me, my dear; business, as
usual," she confided to Mary, when they were
together for a few minutes. "I have made
some money for you, little friend, this time, as
well as for our two darlings. Did you read the

accounts of the money market this week? I suppose not; you never do; but there has been a rise in copper. I have sold out those last investments I made for you, at a capital profit; now you are in something new."

"How clever you are! what a wonderful woman!" exclaimed Mary, gratefully. "Still, I do pity you, dear, passing all your time in brokers' offices; it must be so hot and stifling in the City this weather."

"I never said I passed *all* my time in business," returned Stella, brusquely.

She was, in her own way, a reserved woman since her widowhood, and grew more so every year, as Mary noticed.

Perhaps, thought the latter, Stella had suffered so much from John Morice's suspicious treatment during the last months of his life, that it made her later almost sullen in her reticence as to the smallest details of her movements. Otherwise, no friend could be sweeter-tempered, gayer, more generous both as to money and in leaving Mary free as air to govern the little household at Willow Lea.

Luckily Mary was so sunny natured, and so

busy in body, hands, heart, and brain, from morning till night, that she had no time to be curious. She only held her breath, so to speak, at her friend's wonderful cleverness; respected Stella's reserve that tacitly forbade inquisitiveness; and had never been so happy in all her life as during these years. Still, tears came sometimes into Mary's dove-like eyes when her benefactress occasionally disclosed unhappy, morbid moods, as on the last night when she had been at home.

Not that Mary Dawson was one of the narrow-minded, good persons who are anxious to drive all sheep into their own fold, and think no other pen safe. No; she once heard of a Mohammedan saying, "God made many nations, and gave to each its own book," and she rejoiced thereat. She had read likewise, or gathered somehow, a Hindoo fragment of belief, "Heaven has many doors." Such chance seeds of thought having been planted in her mind, she hardly knew by what means, or when, they found therein kindly soil and grew up. Only, Mary did not say all she thought at the Rectory.

As usual the faithful guardian seized the opportunity of her charges' absence to sketch hastily all that had happened during this last fortnight.

"I am happy to say Pansy's stranger must have really gone away. As you wished, I have watched her closely without her knowing it, and she has seen no one. All is safe."

"That is good news. She is only a child, after all, and so delicate and sensitive in mind that I would not have her ruffled by speaking openly. You may relax your vigilance now. If she guessed we watched her it might teach her to be deceptive."

"She is rather fond of secresy by nature," remarked Mary. "You know that?"

"Yes, it is some little inherited habit; she probably cannot help herself," returned the mother, philosophically.

"But why, I wonder?" asked Mary, aloud. "Rose is as frank as noonday; and you yourself, at school, used to be daring in your pranks, Stella, and say you preferred to take your punishment honestly rather than condescend to hoodwink the teachers."

"True; but I always liked my own way—as I do now, and go it," returned Stella, shutting her lips tightly.

Mary was silenced a moment.

"I have my own ideas of heredity," went on Stella, hurriedly, in a quick, explanatory undertone. "Remember that when Pansy was born I was far from happy; I was hampered in my freedom. No wild bird could beat its wings more desperately against the bars of a cage than I did. Some women have the cage-bird nature. I have not, and Pansy is the same. Let us leave her alone, and she will do no more harm than a young swallow."

So that was settled.

Stella took up the thread of talk more gaily again.

"And otherwise all goes well with my two pets?"

"Well as heart could wish. Rose is always good; always sweet-tempered. What she is to-day you may feel sure she will be to-morrow. Pansy, as usual, has her wayward freaks and fancies, just to keep me from feeling dull, as she says. Still, the child's whims generally have some sense in them. Fancy, lately I began to think she was careless in her appearance, and she used to be so dainty about her dress. So when I caught her crumpling her best hat down on her head with both hands, I was very vexed the other day. Then she confided to me her reason. Mrs. Vyner had said that her hat was more becoming than her sister's, and Pansy could not bear to outshine Rose in any way."

"My darling; that is so like her!" Stella drew a long breath. "Sometimes my own idolatry of that child terrifies me. Do you know, I feel afraid to rejoice over possessing her, even in my own heart, lest she might be snatched from me, because—— Well, well, if Heaven means to show me mercy, I hope to die first; but in any case I could certainly not survive her long."

She spoke hoarsely, from emotion. But Mary thought it best not to notice such exaggerated language. Instead she hastened to change the topic, and began with a cheerful, prosaic air.

"There is just one thing I want to urge

—you will say I am always hammering at the same nail. *Could* you not bring out your daughters into society under your own wing? Think of the pleasure of it! Give up a little of your town cares and business, dear. Really "—with a look of comical dismay—" the charge of your jewels quite frightens me. What experience have I of the world? While you—— "

" While I was sick of it long ago—surfeited. How can I be more here? You do not know how I am trammelled." Mrs. Dean's brow grew black as with a thundercloud, her hands slightly trembled. " I know they are best with you, believe me, and if you never had much society before, my good soul, that is all the more reason why you should enjoy it now. As to their up-bringing—my own was such a failure that I have tried to make theirs exactly the opposite. My childhood was unhappy, soured; our home miserable. Then I was none the better for my school life. Many girls are not, although any evil you met there, Mary, ran off your mind, I own, like rain from a cabbage leaf. No, no; my plan has answered well, believe me. Look at them now, out there, as happy and innocent as a pair of kittens playing together."

And Stella, smiling, if still darkly, her late gloom hardly dissipated, glanced out of the window. The two slim girls on the lawn were teasing and rallying each other as they fired by turns with a saloon pistol at a tiny target fastened to a tree. Frank Vyner stood by, laughing at their efforts. For, try as they would, he made bull's-eyes with ease, while they hardly ever hit the inner circle.

"What of him?" queried the mother, significantly.

"I think it will come right," hazarded Mary, with sober hope. "If not, Rose is too sensible and healthy-minded a girl to grieve much for what is not hers."

And so these two guardians were at ease in their minds.

*   *   *   *   *

Then came an evening when Pansy, whose feet never failed to make a daily pilgrimage to the paddock gate, started back as she approached it; stood still. She was thrilled by waves of emotion pulsing through her with violent heart-beats.

A branch of willow was stuck in the hasp of the gate.

CHAPTER X.

"I love thee as a fountain leaps to light,
I can do nothing else."

"MY fair Barbara Allen! So you have been watching and waiting? You believed I would come?"

"I believed in you. Yes. You promised."

Craigdarrock did not speak again just then, but looked long and attentively at the eloquent face upraised towards his in the twilight. Its features were almost transparent, so to speak; they revealed so clearly the great joyousness, the extraordinary happiness that flooded Pansy's inner being. She forgot inborn coquetry, maidenly shyness; all other feelings were drowned awhile in that deep, overwhelming wave of happy emotion which engulfed and carried her away.

Gently, slowly, Craigdarrock raised to his lips

the soft hand he held, with as devout an air of homage as if doing reverence to his Sovereign Lady at Buckingham Palace.

The simple, vain little heart of her fluttered, swelled with pride, beneath Pansy's girlishly simple bodice. His action pleased her better by far than any more extravagant words or lover-like acts. She seemed to be placed thereby upon a throne, and entreated to condescend with dignity from her all-powerful position.

Five minutes ago, whilst standing dumbstruck at the gate with eager eyes and attentive ears, though hearing, seeing no sound or sign of her companion at the trysting-place, a faint, unusual scent had reached the milk-white maiden's dainty nostrils. She sniffed once, then again. Yes, it was the scent of a cigar, stronger than the fragrance of the new-mown hay still scattered over the meadow. Pansy slipped through the gate noiselessly, then advanced with cautious footsteps on the grass under the thick hedgerow that shadowed the lane.

There a man was, sitting on a log. It was Craigdarrock.

Stirred by some vague sense of presence, the sitter turned his head ; then with a low exclamation sprang up and came forward to meet the slender figure that was moving towards him, presenting a shadowy, nearly ghostly white silhouette against the darkness of the high hedges and overarching trees.

"It is you ; I almost took you for a spirit," were Craigdarrock's first words.

And now they two were standing in the hazel wood on the further side of the grassy lane. Sometimes a labouring man or two, a few gipsies, would pass by that way, but in the wood they were almost utterly safe from any jealous eyes or intruding footsteps.

"You see, I have kept my promise; I have come down here for a few days," went on Craigdarrock, smiling, as their slow footsteps halted at last in a tiny glade set round closely by a hazel copse, while the higher trees receded a little space and left a glimpse of evening sky.

"Ah!"

Pansy's answer was a note of disappointed pain. It sounded through the twilight stillness as if a bird had been startled. The man was surprised, and stood listening what was to follow.

"Why can one never be quite happy for more than a few moments, I wonder?" asked the girl, looking with large, reproachful gaze around on the pearl-grey sky, the thick green undergrowth, and the distant vistas of blue rolling country, descried through leafy gaps, as if she took nature to blame. "I was perfectly happy till you said that. Now you have reminded me that you must go away again."

A flush of pleasure lighted up Craigdarrock's face. He jerked away his cigar—till now he had continued smoking, after due apologies and leave graciously granted, because he had just begun it when Pansy appeared. He made a quick movement closer. As yet he had not touched the silent form that thrilled nevertheless at his near presence. Now he put out his arm, almost encircling her shoulders, and so rested his hand upon a branch. It was well-nigh a caress, and he saw that Pansy was fluttered, therefore he must be gentle, for to

judge by the heavenly rosy blood, ebbing and
dying in soft blushes on her cheeks, she might
easily dart away in a moment from his side,
scared to flight.

"Then you will be sorry when I say 'farewell'?" he murmured in tones that might
have lured a bird from the tree. "Dear little
friend, Blue-eyes, Bright-eyes! You little
know how often in my dreams those eyes of
yours have haunted me, drawn me irresistibly
back to this sequestered nook by the river.
Only for them I should be over the sea, and
far away in Norway by this time. . . . So,
even a minute ago, you would not have been
glad had you known the whole truth. Does
it not teach us a lesson that to be happy it is
sometimes best not to know too much?"

"Yes, I dare say it is so."

Sage seventeen—seventeen years and two
days, so please you!—was ready to agree to
any philosophical proposition her hero might
advance.

So the man and maid, though not declared
lovers yet to each other's ears, looked in each
other's eyes as lovers do, with snatches of

murmured talk. Out of all which sweet parleying one fact rose distinctly—that they were to meet on the morrow to pass a long summer's day together.

"The others," as Pansy vaguely termed her aunt and sister, were bound with some friends on a picnic to a great country place some miles away; then she, left alone, could simply drift a mile down stream, where Craigdarrock should meet her. There was a backwater there, where the reeds grew out of the quiet stream as high as a man, and if a boat were pushed among them with might and main, only a dragon-fly, skimming by like a living blue dart, might see two figures in it; or perhaps a lark that had fluttered up from the green pasture into the blue overhead, singing its soul out in ecstasy till, its hymn of gladness ended, it should drop, no longer a blithe spirit, but a mere feathered fowl, back on the grassy bosom of mother earth.

It was growing late now. Twice Pansy turned her head anxiously towards the lane.

As for Craigdarrock, he had sworn in his own heart that already, this evening, he must

win a reward from her sweet virginal lips for
his having thrown aside society's pleasures,
duties, business, and broken all manner of small
ties in freeing himself to come thither.   All
day he had thought himself a fool for his pains.
Imagine a man of the world, a man of his age,
caring so greatly for a mere passing flirtation
with a romantic bread-and-butter miss!   Nay,
not that.   This was a young woodland nymph,
a water-nixie, a spirit-creature of no ordinary
flesh and blood, whose large eyes looked at
him with such innocent surprise and gladness
in his presence, as that which newly created
Eve might have shown to Adam.

Knowing, alas! only too well how to woo
a woman, Craigdarrock whispered his request
pleadingly—then met with a rapid success that
surprised himself.

Pansy certainly hesitated at first.   In all
her brief life she did not remember kissing
any man, though many were the embraces she
showered on her mother and sister and aunt.
But, after all, why not?   Towards them it was
such a simple thing, a real token of affection.
Then, where lay any difference in likewise

thanking this her only friend for coming so far to see her?

So deciding, Pansy raised her face suddenly with a child's quick obedience, brushing a rough portion of cheek near his ear with her lips, soft as an opening rose, in awkward haste. Craigdarrock laughed in his heart; he had thought as much, and was satisfied. Then he took her small white face between his two hands, framed it in the hollow of his palms, and so, after one long look in her luminous eyes, kissed her mouth softly, lingeringly. From head to foot the girl was thrilled with a strange, new sensation. Hitherto she had loved this man in fancy, in mind, with her vivid imagination; but now the woman's heart in her body answered to his mute call as her master henceforth.

" *Tu whit! tu whoo!* " An owl hooted from somewhere amid the dark sepia-coloured masses of tree-tops beyond them.

"Oh, that is unlucky," lamented Pansy, under her breath, with superstitious awe.

"He is only a watchman of the night, telling us it is time to part," Craigdarrock consoled her. "Good night, my pet. I wish I dared keep you to say more good nights; but for your own sweet sake I must be wise."

They parted by the gate in the lane. Slowly, seeming more like a spirit than ever, the slim young girl in her white gown glided away through the meadow, where clouds of grey night-moths fluttered up in the twilight from the grasses, roused by her brushing feet.

Craigdarrock watched her till she vanished; then his face changed. He lit a fresh cigar, and with a frown turned moodily up the lane.

*   *   *   *   *

The third evening since Craigdarrock first came to the hazel grove was darkening over the woods, and gleaming with afterglow reflections on the river. Grown bolder now, the sweethearts were standing under a chestnut tree, of which the branches made a large-leafed roof; and to this bower a path, used only by woodcutters and gamekeepers, wound through the coppice. It was the third evening, and the last! For Craigdarrock had just broken the news to his little sweetheart that he must return to London next day. His brief visit here had been an idyll, a charming pastoral idyll; he should never forget it. But there were matters he must see to—business; a shooting-party in Scotland to be arranged; his Norway trip finally decided.

Pansy, listening, felt a hot soreness in her breast, a pain there she had never known before, except after bodily exertion; for her heart from infancy was subject to these attacks.

"But you are coming back again?" she beseechingly murmured, ashamed to show how sharply she suffered, seeing *he* was so strangely unmoved. How could a man seem to love her thus dearly one moment, the next speak without wincing of their parting—perhaps, nay surely! for weary months?

"Yes, oh yes. I must return some day. I shall see you again; either when you are 'come out' in London or here," Craigdarrock hesitatingly replied. He was thinking in his heart it might be best, after all, if he were to go away to-morrow and see her sweet little face never more.

Then an unexpected sound close by made them both start apart.

CHAPTER XI.

"To mould denial to a pleasing shape
    In all things, and most specially in love,
    Is a hard task ; . . .
    . . . Cunning is the maid
    That can convert a lover to a friend."

" *Yap! yap! yap!* "

A dog's approaching bark along the path
had disturbed the lovers. Next moment the
white-and-tan body of a fox terrier wriggled
into view, nose down, scenting along their late
footsteps.

"It is Crab, Frank Vyner's dog," whispered
Pansy, in eager caution. "Go out of sight,
please! I will try and send him away."

She hurried forward, followed by the dog,
bounding upon her and licking her hands.
Then, composing herself to a sedate air, though
with tears not far from her eyes, and bitter

wrath in her heart, she came full upon Frank himself round a curve of the path.

The young man was in evening dress, over which he wore a light coat, and he was strolling along with his hands in the pockets of the latter, with a set, unusually moody look upon his face.

"Good evening, Miss Pansy. It is quite a surprise to find you here. May I ask if you have been alone in the wood?" he blurted out suddenly, as he stopped, with an ill attempt at an awkward laugh, and a jealous look of suspicion spoiling his merry blue eyes.

"You may not."

Pansy's head lifted itself proudly on her long throat; two crimson roses blossomed out magically on her cheeks; her eyes, in their turn, flashed summer lightnings.

"I saw you a little while ago come slipping down along the river by the willows," went on the young man, with a darksome air. "I was standing up the lane watching, though you did not see me. You looked all about, and then darted across the path into the wood, as if you were in a tremendous hurry. So I—did not

know what was up. I "—he stammered and
nearly broke down—" I thought I might come
and see."

" You were spying !"

The accusation, though uttered with soft
scorn, was hurled so straight in his face that
Vyner started back as if the girl had struck
him. Both glowered at each other for two
angry moments.

"I was doing nothing of the kind," then
returned the young man, loftily. "But as that
is your opinion of me, perhaps I had better go.
Good evening."

He set his face to a wonderful sternness,
considering how round and ruddy it was by
rights, squared his shoulders, and stepped deeper
into the wood.

" Come back ! Do not go that way ! " cried out
Pansy, imperiously as a little queen.

Frank stopped dead, and looked at her in
sulky doubt.

"Why not ?—unless you have come out to
meet some other fellow, although I cannot
guess who it may have been. Why should you
stop me ?"

" Who is there I should be likely to meet ? "
inquired naughty Pansy, feigning a light laugh,
and drawing him back by the witching gleam
in her eyes. " Who? Now think! Tell me !"

" How should I know ?"

Frank had grumpily returned, and was now
moving slowly beside his sovereign mistress
back to the lane. Pansy's smile was upon him,
exorcising the demons that jealous love had
called to come in and make their habitation in
his heart. Oh, she could twist him round her
little finger ! That he owned to himself; and
perhaps she knew it, though he was not sure of
having gained her real liking in the least yet.
There was a sandy-haired, smooth-faced youth
reading with a tutor in the village. Likewise
the tutor himself, an underbred, clever individual, who read Greek plays for amusement, and
smoked a short black pipe. There were also an
ascetic curate, supposed to be vowed to celibacy,
and—and one or two others of male kind
scattered about the neighbourhood.

Pansy laughed at his suspicions of each and
all with sweet scornfulness. There was not a
man among them, and he knew it, she airily

jeered. And she had as yet spoken to none of these—not one. Frank was her friend, she hoped, the friend of all of the Willow Lea household, so she did not wish to quarrel with him; but he must trust her, and if he went back through the wood that would not be trust, and she would never speak to him again.

Whereupon Miss Pansy passed through the paddock-gate, and shut it with a click.

"I forbid you to come through here," she said regally, with a farewell nod.

Frank gripped the top rail, which was a high one, with both hands. Pansy had just turned away when she gave one look over her shoulder, twisting her slender neck, merely to see how this foolish squire took his dismissal. She beheld his body in the horizontal position of vaulting over the gate, and, alas! reminding her wickedly of a counter-jumper. Next moment he stood beside her, upright, obstinate, and impenitent.

"Forgive me! You did not say I might not *come over*."

His cruel fair tried to frown with severity, but the corners of her mouth relaxed, despite herself, into a smile. At that her faithful follower took courage, and his tongue ran away with him.

Frank feared she was still angry; that she had not fully forgiven him. Would she not say she did forgive; graciously receive his assurances that never again would he so offend? Indeed, he had not been spying; only for two days he had not once seen her, and so kept hanging about all the afternoon in vain, if she would believe it, to catch one glimpse——

But Pansy had taken alarm. She was annoyed, scared, and was just slipping by the hedge to escape, when Frank effectually barred the way by dropping on one knee, and catching at her gown with trembling hands.

"Do not go! Only just listen! Pansy—one word, please!"

"I cannot stay, I cannot! Why can you not say anything you have got to tell me to-morrow, when you come to play tennis? It is too late this evening, really, Mr. Vyner."

"You always laugh at me at Willow Lea. You *won't see!* you never give me a chance," went on the victim, abjectly.

Pansy made two impatient steps, though he still held her gown with reverent finger-tips. Poor Frank would not rise, so dropped forlornly on both knees, and dragged himself after her through the dewy grass, still pleading.

"Oh, get up. Please *do!*" insisted Pansy, in her turn, suddenly laughing wildly, with a burst of such unrestrained mirth that even Frank, although heart-sore, was infected by its gaiety.

"There! look at your knees! two wet patches! Why, you are expected to go up to the old Miss Wisemans' on the hill for a round game of cards, with jelly handed round in glasses, and lemonade, are you not? You told me so yesterday. My sister and aunt went half an hour ago. You will be late."

"Oh! never mind the old ladies and their round game;" Frank had nearly used a stronger word of setting at naught. "Say you *do* forgive me."

"Yes, yes. Of course I do. *Now go!*"

Away skimmed Pansy, light-footed, over the field. Not till she had reached the screening shelter of the shrubbery did she relax that

presently breathless flight. Then she suddenly
stopped short; a troubled look, increasing
rapidly to passionate grief, overspread her
extremely variable features. Her eyebrows
took a melancholy droop, and her lips were
pressed unusually close together, while the
late scene rose first in her mind.

She had said to Frank, "Go!" but would
fain have added, "Go, and be nice to Rose."
What a pity one can so seldom say what one
really thinks! such as, for instance, "See here,
Frank Vyner, my sister cares for you; I do
not. Be sensible; make her happy, and then
without doubt you will be happy too." Oh,
how vexing it was that this Jack would not
follow after his own true Jill! It did seem too
bad that Frank should come teasing in this
way. It was just contrariety; for Pansy could
assure herself quite honestly that she had
never coquetted with this man in the slightest
degree, though it was her natural bent to do
so with the few others she had ever seen. No;
loyalty to Rose forbade the faintest promptings
towards any such, even momentary treachery.

As Pansy stood panting after her run, the

sudden pain she had felt in the wood, that had been lying in wait in her mind meanwhile, once more hurt her breast with a sharp bodily pang.

Alas! alas! Craigdarrock would be gone to-morrow, and he had not even said, "Good-bye."

A gush of tears welled out from the azure eyes, that had never since childhood known such a bitter flood. They were very fountains of Mara; but the flow of grief was a relief. While the pretty sufferer pressed her slender hands over her heart, alone fighting back the attack that generally caused such sympathy and anxiety to those around her, as she raised her poor little agonized face to the night sky, there came a quick step on the other side of the thick yew hedge separating the shrubbery from the high-road; two notes were repeated in a low, seemingly careless whistle. In sudden joy, Pansy, almost doubting her happy ears, managed with trembling lips to answer by the same notes whistled in reverse order. Then something was flung over the hedge and fell on the gravel at her feet.

The missile was a scrap of paper wrapped

round a small stone. She caught at it eagerly,
unfolded it, but in the twilight could not read
the words, though she knew whose hand must
just now have pencilled them. Cheered again,
the childish soul paused, looked round with
eager, turned head, only to hear departing footsteps. Then, spurred by reviving hope, Pansy
hastened towards the drawing-room lights that
gleamed through the glass door she had lately
left ajar. With fluttering heart she stood in
the radius of the lamp and eagerly scanned the
message—

" Meet me ten days from now. I am coming
again.

" Yours,

" C."

Pansy kissed the paper rapturously, re-
peatedly. Hers, hers ! He was hers. She was
sure of it.

Craigdarrock, sauntering cautiously away
through the wood, had espied that little scene
between his rival and lady-love in the meadow.
There and then he determined to come back
and " cut the fellow out." For love alone he

might not have done it; but let jealousy be added, and love becomes angry passion in a man's breast. He must be first. He will not be beaten.

So the days came and went, till once again, and many times more than once, the willow twig was fastened in the gate by preconcerted signal. And Pansy, through her love, had grown to be a woman in soul when she met her lover there. Yet in many ways she was still merely a child.

She puzzled Craigdarrock; her love for him was so ardent, yet frank to transparency. Then, too, she loved so many other beings with bewildering warmth of affection, from her sister and her kitten to every bird that sings.

"Tell me this," he asked her one day, with an intensity of fervour that awed Pansy's susceptible mind almost to fear; and yet he merely assumed it as easily as he put on his hat, out of somewhat cruel curiosity to vivisect this virgin heart, and see its quiverings and inmost hidden core. "Do you love me better than any one else alive or dead?—than everybody else, I say? I must know!"

And Pansy's breath rose in her throat; for she was troubled.

"What will you do when your sister marries?" persisted her tormentor, fixing her with his piercing eyes. "Will that make you very unhappy?"

"No. I shall miss her, but still *she* will be happy."

"Ah! woman's instinct spoke there. And your mother, my sweet? You can endure life now, although you only see her once a week or less often. Perhaps you love her all the better for that. If you should leave her for another home, Pansy, tell me, could you still be happy?"

"Ye-es, if I saw her sometimes."

A thrill of joy, suggested so easily by those words, "another home," had trembled all through the girl's slight frame; yet she spoke doubtfully, for did she not adore her darling mother? Still the brilliant eyes half a head above her burned their light into her own. Then the voice, to which the whole of her inner being vibrated in exquisite sympathy, went on in deeper, solemn tones—

" But what if you never saw *me* again after
this day ? "

" *I should die !* "

The slender arms relaxed, untwined themselves from about her lover's neck, dropped
by her side like loosened ivy from a tree.
Pansy's head drooped ; she shivered uncon-
trollably, so that Craigdarrock was frightened
at his own experiment—she turned so white.

" You did not think I really meant it ? No,
no ! There ! "—cried the lover, in hasty com-
punction. He pressed burning kisses on his
pet's cold lips, caressed her with tenderest en-
dearments till the breath of his love revived
the faint form like strong wine, was as balm to
the wounded spirit. " We must not part *yet—
not just yet*," was the thought that froze the
man's own heart like ice. But it seemed too
cruel to utter it then ; and he only spoke joyful
reassurances to console his white angel, his
blue-eyed queen, his spirit-love, that must not
fade away into mist and moonbeams.

It was enough to make Pansy happy again.
He loved her ! so, trusting him utterly, she left
the future to his care.

CHAPTER XII.

"This is the porcelain clay of humankind."

HOT weather. The hottest June it was that
had been known for years in England.

Willow Lea, lying low in its nook by the
river, was bathed at early morn in the sun's
first rays, baked at noontide, and through most
of the day resembled a dumb thing gasping for
breath, with its blinds drawn closely down and
windows open. Only when the clock chiming
in the grey church tower of the village pro-
claimed evening, when the air was cooler and
shadows longer, the blinds drew up, life in the
little house revived, and two girlish voices
resounded in calls and answers to each other.

"You are both like the birds in the shrubbery,
beginning to chirp, and hopping about over the
lawn after being drowsy all day," said Mary
Dawson.

"Ah! I wish there would come one grey day," answered Pansy. "Just one of those gentle, cloudy days when one seems living in a half-dream. I am so tired of the blinding light and the sharp black shadows."

Pansy had grown even more exquisitely pale than usual, while the blue veins showed in her forehead, delicately traced, and there were dark circles round her eyes that seemed to make these larger than ever. She hardly ate at all, started, turning rosy red, at the least sound— the click of the gate, the tap of a rose branch on the window. Yet her lips were always lightly curved, as if a smile lay sleeping there, ready to be roused at the slightest call; and to the affectionate inquiries of the others she would answer, as if awaking from a happy day-dream, that she was "quite well, very well;" only the heat had tired her just a little one day, given her a tiny headache the next.

"You used to say you worshipped King Sol," observed Mary, puzzled.

"So do flowers love the sun, and yet, see, they are hanging their heads too," came in soft answer.

For the roses in the garden were drooping
or over-blown in that early sultry July, and
the hedgerow flowers were smothered with the
white dust that lay inches deep in the lanes.
A new light had come into Pansy's great blue
eyes of late—a sweet one of tenderness for all
around her, for the meanest insect in her path.
Her foster-mother noticed that she was even
gentler, more lovable, than ever before in her
caressing ways.   Yet Mary Dawson felt
almost sorry to see the change. For Pansy's
childish spirit of mischief and harmless malice
had folded its wings. It only revived when
she railed against Frank Vyner in her old
way, that no more hurt than if a child were
to pelt one with daisies.

And Rose? She, good girl, was so healthy
in body, so evenly sweet-tempered in mind,
never did winter's cold or summer's heat affect
her. Yet her pleasant face was sobered, faint
hopes in her heart were sadly dulled by mis-
givings. She was apparently so assiduous at
her painting, no one liked to disturb her; she
spent long hours practising on the piano, yet
the sounds from the latter were listless, and

repeated monotonously. Then one morning
Mary Dawson, happening to glance at the
sketch on Rose's easel, saw it had progressed
very slowly, and exclaimed unthinkingly—

"Why, dear, what has happened? Your
paper is spotted here and there, as if it had
been caught in a rain-shower."

"I must have spilled some water on it,"
explained Rose, growing very red. "I—I was
watering the plants yesterday."

"What a daylight owl I am! She has been
crying," guessed Mary, suddenly enlightened,
and her heart was sore for the girl who was
dearest to her.

It was this little woman's nature to care
most for the disregarded ones of this world
—the ugly, the sick, the of-no-account. Her
heart was so full of pity for these that she
had become a make-weight in life.

"Of course," as Mary soliloquized to herself,
with silently speaking lips and dilating eyes,
as was a trick of hers when alone—"of course,
Pansy is her mother's heart's dearest, the idol
Stella worships in secret. And there is Frank
Vyner, when he calls—and he does invent

wonderful excuses for calling — he always
follows Pansy with his eyes as if he was a
child's toy swan swimming in a basin of water,
and she the horse-shoe magnet held over its
edge. All the same, he talks to Rose by the
hour, and seems the best of friends with her.
I suppose because he needs other consolation,
for Pansy is so utterly indifferent to him.
Why, last week, when he said, ' Good-bye,'
the child was so absent-minded she answered,
' How do you do?' quite sweetly. Well, it is
natural in men to be taken through the eyes;"
and Miss Dawson philosophically went on tying
covers on her jam-pots. " What bother they do
give! Here we are with the cottage still unlet,
because Stella hopes on he will propose."

Nevertheless, Pansy's subtle smile and unconscious fascination would almost have cap-
tured Mary's most devoted and entire heart's
allegiance at times, but that the guardian repeated to herself obstinately, with a spice of
contrariety—

" Come, come; why, an honest milkmaid
ought to be as interesting to any fair-minded
person as a beautiful princess. A homely

candle can only burn its best; and it cannot help not being a silver lamp."

So Mary alone, in the little house and their small environing circle, loved Rose best.

What of Rose herself? All her young life, since her baby-sister was shown her, she had adored Pansy as an ideal self—the one half of her that was loveliest, most gifted, best. Hitherto she had hardly ever hidden a thought in her heart from her bright soul-twin. But now—— Ah! she must keep her secret. If, indeed, the man she loved cared most for Pansy —and who could help it?—then in time Pansy surely *must* love him too, although now she only laughed at him. Not a shadow must cloud that happy future.

No one knew, when Rose sat alone in the schoolroom, how often her eyes were lifted from her sketch with wistful glances into the far-away. Then, if there came the sound of a rider trotting down the lane, she could not help starting and listening intently. Frank Vyner often rode, and it might be he.

One day Rose heard horse's hoofs which stopped at the back entrance. With trembling haste the young girl smoothed her hair, gave a hasty glance in the mirror, and slipped downstairs with short breath and a beating heart. The drawing-room door, however, remained fast shut, instead of opening to admit a manly presence and cheery voice. A quarter of an hour passed, then Rose timidly rang the bell in secret desperation.

"Who rode up just now? I thought, perhaps, the—the doctor might have stopped?" she inquired hesitatingly of the maid who answered the summons.

"No, miss; it was the butcher's boy."

Rose gave herself, figuratively, a good shaking; mentally scolded that silly, sentimental fool, Rose Dean. It was unmaidenly, immodest, to keep thinking about a man who was just her good friend, nothing more. Still, the tears did rise to her eyes with a smarting sense of disappointment.

And all the while, Pansy, wrapped in her secret happiness, had only one inner regret— that she must not confide in Rose. At least, Craigdarrock had said, "Not yet." And his manner was so gently persuasive, yet com-

manding, that small wonder her shyly hinted
request died on her lips in his kiss.

Pansy saw that her dear elder self was
troubled too. "It is because Frank Vyner is
so slow in his courting," decided sage seventeen, impatient with so laggard a lover after
her own vivid experience. But it will all come
right, I know. Oh, I know! Only I must
hold aloof, and not vex her by seeming to notice
anything."

It was odd that Pansy, with all her quickness, never seemed to perceive how often
Frank's gaze rested on herself in long glances
of admiration. She did not see, because she
herself would be looking at the darkening river
with a dreaming expression. She did not think
of him, because her mind was busy elsewhere,
none around her guessing what picture was in
her mental vision. But she was musing of
the thick hazel copse down yonder, where she
wandered on those evenings when the others
were in the village. Or she was again in a
punt up the backwater, where the flags grew
so tall and thick that the boat, once pushed in
among them, was hidden so close by that green

upright army, with its downward-hanging leaves like pennons, that no jealous eyes could espy the two that were in it. She saw a manly handsome face looking close at her own. Words of love were whispered again in her ears, making the noises of common life around her seem to come from a distance, as if she was living in the land of shadows, and that reality, actual blessed life, lay only there—in those scenes that had been.

She was remembering yesterday. She was thinking of to-morrow.

CHAPTER XIII.

" Pan loved his neighbour Echo ; but that child
　Of Earth and Air pined for the Satyr leaping ;
　The Satyr loved, with wasting madness wild,
　　The bright nymph Lyda ; and so the three went
　　　weeping.
　As Pan loved Echo, Echo loved the Satyr,
　　The Satyr Lyda ; and so the three went weeping."

THERE came an evening when, after the day's
drought, the sky grew suddenly blackened as
the twilight. fell.

So dark it grew and so quickly that Pansy,
who had wandered outside alone after supper,
was alarmed.　She had turned into the churchyard near the river—one of her favourite haunts.
A strange place for this fair young creature of
seventeen to choose in which to stroll, smiling
gently at secret fancies.　But Pansy loved the
quiet of the spot, with its great environing
elms in which the rooks cawed ; and its green
waves of sward, with here and there a rosebush

blowing, or a giant yew spreading. Graves roused no memories in her of a vanished presence. The dead slept well there under the daisies, was her vague thought. When one died, some far-off day, it would be sweet to rest here; while the broad river went gliding by under the overhanging chestnut trees, the pride of the village, that glassed themselves greenly in its stream.

But now a sudden flash of lightning from out the darkness overhead made Pansy start back, with dazzled eyes.

Cr-a-a-sh!—a loud thunder-clap followed almost immediately, with a roar as of heaven's weightiest artillery. Before its reverberations had died away into distant mutterings, Pansy was speeding up the flagged path bordered with lilacs to the church porch.

The church door stood open; for so the rector liked to keep it till late in the evenings. "How could the village folk, or chance strangers, think and pray on a week-day unless they could be sure of some quiet spot?" he was wont to say.

So Pansy darted in and fled straight to the chancel rails, where she sank down panting on the cushions of the step. A second peal rumbled terrifically. It seemed just over the roof; but, with a sense of having taken holy sanctuary, Pansy only nestled closer and felt safe. How dark it was! The familiar stained windows showed mysteriously dim; elsewhere all was deep gloom. Then came a swishing noise of rain, and while she listened, in a reverie that was almost luxurious, minutes passed.

At last, at the sound of light footsteps in the stillness, Pansy raised her head. They came slow and faltering up the aisle, nearer and nearer, then stopped. Hidden by the intervening pulpit, Pansy could discern no figure from her lowly nook, but she held her breath to listen. Some one else seemed listening too.

Then two whispers crossed in the gloom—

" Pansy ! "

" Rose ! "

The sisters appeared to have divined each other's presence by some inner sense, which never struck either as strange.

" Come here, and sit beside me," said Pansy, softly.

Rose came forward in doubt.

"What! Here? It seems—too sacred."

"Why?" asked Pansy, in a wondering tone, clear as that of a little child. "If we say no harm, and think none, why should we not sit here? I always do when I come by myself."

So Rose sat down at her junior's bidding, drawing her skirts aside.

"The rain was so wetting; you might take cold by touching me."

Pansy for all reply put her arms about her sister in a loving embrace. Rose apprehended the hidden meaning of the action, which was that they two loved to share their smallest pleasures and troubles; and her chilled body felt comforted. Their two young heads drew nearer, then fondly rested cheek against cheek. The storm went on outside, with thunder that still rumbled, and lightning-flashes instantaneously illumining the dark interior of the church, while sheets of rain hissed down as from open floodgates. But the two sisters sat silent.

All at once Pansy withdrew her face slightly.

"Rose, you are crying. Your cheek is wet. Oh, my dear!"

" It is nothing—indeed ! "

Rose softly wiped her eyes in the darkness, sorely ashamed. Then she felt Pansy's warm kiss, and heard a whisper of sisterly love.

" I know ; I understand."

A pause followed between the two girls for a few seconds. Next Rose answered, trying to cheer up.

" It is wicked of me to feel—so ! especially here. Don't mind me, darling. He cares for you most. And I am—I shall be quite content."

" But I do not care for Frank at all except insomuch as I hoped he loved you !" returned Pansy, horror-struck at the thought. Her tone was so clearly truthful, that its sound cheered Rose like glad music. " Oh, believe me, it will all come right. *I know it will!* He will ask you some day to be his wife."

" You really think so ? "

Pansy could feel the thrill of happiness that electrified poor Rose. The latter murmured in a last protest almost inaudible, low though their previous whispers were.

" But are you quite certain you would not

care for him later—if we were both convinced it
is you that he really liked best all the time?
For if so——"

"Never! never!"

"Yet you own he is so good and kind! I
wonder at it."

"Because——"

The secret was on Pansy's very lips, about
to be revealed. At last surely the moment had
come when the wonderful tale of Craigdarrock's
romantic wooing might be imparted to her
other self. Rose would never tell—till she was
given leave.

"Because——"

At that very instant there was a sound of
stamping in the porch, and Frank Vyner's
matter-of-fact voice called into the church—

"Are you there?"

The two girls, startled, pressed closer, but
with a spice of mischief kept quiet.

"I know you are there, so you may as well
answer," went on the young man, coming into
the aisle. "Miss Dawson is in a terrible fright
lest you might have been drowned in the rain,
so I offered to bring your waterproofs."

"Yes; here we are," said two sweet voices in unison; and Pansy added—

"Let us come to the porch and watch the rain."

Both felt it would be desecration to speak with Frank inside the church of common things. To tell each other of the most secret love in the heart of each was different. That was a holy confidence fit for such a sacred place.

The big rain-drops came hissing down and rebounding from the flagged path, while hail-stones whitened the grass. There was more light now to see, for westward the darkness of clouds had parted, seeming to open wide gleaming portals in a prison vault.

Frank, looking at the sisters, inwardly thought both were like sweet spirits standing together under the Norman arch of the church door, but Pansy the most seraphic. He offered to put on her cloak first, but somehow the angelic pair avoided him and helped each other.

"How could you tell we were here?" asked Rose, diffidently.

"Well, I guessed that at all events one of you might be, for I have often seen *you* come here." And Frank turned, as he could not often help doing, his gaze on the girlish face that looked so pale and lustrous-eyed in the twilight. He added hastily, in awkward apology, "But I never have interrupted you, have I, Miss Pansy, although I knew it?"

"No," said Pansy, indifferently.

Rose shivered, and Frank at once remarked it, fearing she had got a chill. He advised their starting home for her sake, with such genuine kindness that a gentle glow warmed the girl's humble heart once more.

Meanwhile more anxious searchers for these two strayed lambs from the fold were out in various directions. Gardener George was stumbling up and down the uneven pavement of the village side-path, making inquiries of the chemist and grocer, that ended, on his own account, in the Blue Lion public-house. They met a maid with more wraps, picking her steps down the lane.

Mary Dawson herself was peering out on all sides from under the yew tree by the gate, and got scolded and laughed at for her fears.

Lastly, on the door-mat, Sprite was keeping

up a tiny bark, his black little body writhing with expectation, while every now and then he adventured four delicate paws on the wet gravel, only to dart back to the mat in fastidious disgust.

"You darling!" cried Pansy, catching him up with kisses. "Do you know you are to have a new silver collar, with as fine a peal of bells as Miss Rose and I can buy? But it costs a great deal of money, little dog, and we have to work so hard—so hard."

"We have to sew house-linen, and mark, and mend, and get paid by auntie; and she is such a rigid taskmistress," chimed in Rose.

"Is it true?" asked Frank. "Why not ask your mother to give Sprite a collar?"

"*It is for her!*—her birthday present," both cried out.

"If we bought it out of the pocket-money she gives us, that would be only giving back her own," added Pansy, loftily.

"But it is very slow work," owned Rose.

"Do, please, do let me help!" cried Frank, with beseeching eagerness. "I should be so proud to be allowed to join in Mrs. Dean's

present. Will you? You know I am quite
an old friend now."

"Oh—I do think—don't you think he
might?" hesitated Rose, but with sparkling
eyes, deprecatingly consulting her junior by a
glance.

Pansy had not the heart to refuse, yet was
vexed. This present to their mother was no
careless gift. *She* had first been inspired by
the idea that it should be the wages of their
own labour, a token of real sacrifice and love.
If Frank joined them, the significance of the
gift was lessened. Ah! if Craigdarrock might
have been a fourth, then she would have felt
no jealousy of poor Frank's request.

So she gaily twitted him, to conceal un-
willingness.

"But you only mean to put your hand in
your pocket and bring out your purse. That
costs you nothing but coin. Sprite's collar has
to be earned, every silver sixpence of it."

"What shall I do, then? Ask my father to
hire me as a labourer to dig the garden? or
shall I black my face and go round the village
with my banjo?" asked Frank, half in jest,

but boyishly eager to gain his end, nevertheless.

"Yes, yes! Go and play the banjo, and hold out your hat! Do! I wish you would! It would be so funny to see you!" cried Pansy, in ecstatic delight.

"Don't! it would be dreadful!" exclaimed Rose, aghast. "*Please* don't! It would be much nicer to dig in the garden. I should hate——" She broke off short.

The idea of her hero grinning for pence, an object of ridicule, was actually painful to her.

CHAPTER XIV.

" Womankind more joy discovers
Making fools than keeping lovers."

THE festival day of the neighbouring village
regatta had come, and was dying away into
the mild stillness of evening. Overhead the
little cloudlets seemed to Pansy's fancy like a
flock of rosy sheep in the blue plain that was
fading to pearl-colour low in the west, while
a mysterious veil darkened slowly over the
east.

The great event had come and gone. But
poor Pansy neither left Willow Lea nor saw
any of the day's fun. In vain Frank Vyner
called early, whizzing through the wooden gate
like a friendly bombshell, as Mary Dawson said,
exploding in eager directions of where to go
and how to see best. She kept silence till he
departed; then, not raising her eyelashes,

merely murmured with a languor that was slightly assumed—

"I do not care to go. It will be very tiring."

"Oh! not go?" likewise murmured Rose in remonstrance. But a slight flush coloured her fresh cheeks, somewhat paler lately than their wont, and she too dropped her eyelids.

"Not go?" echoed Mary Dawson, in secret relief, raising her eyebrows, and assuming a tone of cheerful carelessness. "Well, perhaps you are right, child. You never can stand much heat or fatigue, and it will be a tiring day."

Thus all three pretended not to understand each other. And so Rose left, eager-eyed, in the motherly charge of the plump smiling duenna, who looked like personified Comfort. And Pansy, swinging as high as the swing-ropes would take her among the lime branches, called out, "Enjoy yourselves!" clear as a bird. But once they were well out of sight, she swung slower and slower till her feet touched the ground; and two big tears stood in her eyes.

After all, it was not much of a sacrifice. But she did dearly love the smallest excitement that ever came into their quiet lives. And the gaily dressed crowd, the squeaking of Punch and Judy, even the barrel-organs' music, roused her to delight. The sight of a few soldiers' scarlet coats against the intense green of the river meadows made her almost cry out with pleasure as when the poppies were spread blood-red in great patches in the corn, and she looked at the glory of the fields with eyes ecstatically dilating to take their fill. The rush and swing of oars as the boats raced by, the cheers of the running backers, made her almost weep to her secret shame at being so stirred.

Why, excitement *never* tired her!

Now evening was here, and the holiday pair were returned. But Rose was strangely silent, actually incoherent in her replies. She owned, which was wonderful, that she *did* feel queer, and would like to go straight to bed. Rose to have a headache without cause!—one would as soon expect snow to fall at midsummer!

"It must have been the sun. Yes, come, dear, and I will make you comfortable," clucked Mary Dawson, like a hen calling a drooping chick.

Pansy followed to share her sister's seclusion, as a matter of course. For whenever anything ailed one of these two who loved each other, the other seldom or never left her.

But still more strange! for the first time in her life, Rose, in a smothered voice, her face half buried in the pillow, deprecatingly begged to be left " quite alone."

Slightly astonished, if not rebuffed, Pansy stole away on tiptoe, and, wandering out of doors again, strolled about aimlessly in the gathering dusk.

It did seem hard to have renounced her pleasure without having given any the more to Rose. For Pansy began to suspect that " things had turned crooked," so perhaps it would have made no difference if she herself had gone and enjoyed the fun of the regatta, always hitherto a grand yearly excitement.

Craigdarrock was absent for five days. What leaden days! and how very long! when the skies seemed less blue, nature less fair, and daily duties and usual pleasures had become only a form of watching and waiting till his return. If she could have been of any use to

Rose in there, Pansy would neither have felt dull nor have repined; now, as she softly moved up and down over the lawn and by the shrubbery, the distant sounds of village mirth strangely excited her. She was young and alone.

A house-boat was moored across the river, and from its saloon windows there floated the sounds of a waltz played on a piano. Pansy drew nearer, till at last she approached the wall dividing the rectory garden from the end of that of Willow Lea. There was a tiny orchard here, where five apple trees stood in a grassy strip. Before these came raspberry bushes and rows of pea-hedges, so that the spot was screened from observation. A pale moon was rising yonder; the air was still. The garden wall was high and topped with masses of jasmine.

Tra-ra-ra! lira-la! went the music. Pansy began to dance airily, using a Shetland shawl, bending and waving and weaving a dance of her own, with as natural a grace as the inborn instinct which teaches a kid to skip or a kitten to gambol—stopping now and again in pauses of untaught charm.

When she ceased, flushed and self-pleased,

drawing a long breath, there came unexpected applause.

" Bra-*vo !* " was emphatically whispered from somewhere overhead.

With a great start, Pansy gazed round in astonished indignation. Then her glance rested on the garden wall.

There, framed by the jasmine flowers, and showing in queer contrast to them, was a black face set in a wide shirt-collar ending in two huge points. This diabolic apparition was furthermore rolling the whites of its eyes, and grinning as if the top of its head might open on hinges like an ink-bottle.

The girl on the instant made a movement towards flight, then, remembering that the individual's body must be on the rectory side of the wall, she paused as suddenly. Her large eyes looked back with frightened curiosity, such as might be seen in the beautiful orbs of a hare or a startled doe, inquisitive to note the appearance of a likely enemy, before swiftly flying from danger.

" Don't be afraid! It is me—it is I! Don't you know me, Pansy ? "

The voice was the voice of Frank Vyner, but the face was as black as a mediæval devil or a chimney-sweep.

Pansy drew nearer, hesitating whether to laugh or be horrified.

" I don't believe you."

" But I am, on my honour. So you didn't know me! What a jolly lark! Why, I've been singing and twanging my banjo for the last hour or two at the regatta. *Why didn't you come?* It was you who told me to do it, you know; and I've made twelve and ninepence, honour bright. Not a soul knew who I was! See, Miss Dawson gave me this lucky shilling herself; " and the speaker held up a coin between his finger and thumb with a laugh there was no mistaking, it was so boyishly jolly.

He was seated on the wall now with dangling legs that cruelly kicked at the jasmine tendrils, which strove to oppose his passage.

" Go down! you will be seen by somebody," imperiously dictated Pansy, in a dignified voice.

Frank dropped at once—into the mould of the flower-bed under the wall.

" I said, ' Go ; ' not, ' Come,' " admonished his charmer, laughing despite her commanding air.

" I am so sorry. I did not understand," pleaded the culprit. " But, I say, how jolly it was to see you dance! Do let us have a turn together, you and I. I never have waltzed with you yet."

His arm curled swiftly towards Pansy's waist, though his head dropped in somewhat sheepish entreaty.

Tra-ra-ra! sounded the music once more, in renewed joyousness.

Pansy yielded more to its fascinations than to those of her partner, and away the young pair footed it merrily by themselves on the grass. Frank piloted her between the apple trees, dodged the projecting boughs, guided her young figure round and round the grass plot, till they both stopped from sheer want of breath. Pansy was full of laughter ; but some other emotion was gleaming in the flashing eyeballs set in the coal-black visage that breathed so near her own.

Frank had not withdrawn his arm yet from his partner's waist, which was against the rules

of dancing, as the sylph reflected. Before she
had time to reprimand him, however, the de-
linquent bent his head still nearer to hers,
tightened his hold, and whispered in entreating
accents—

"One kiss, Pansy, darling ! Do let me have
just one—— "

At that Pansy broke violently from his clasp
with almost passionate anger on her face that a
moonbeam partly revealed.

"Don't !" she breathed, in horror-struck de-
fiance, "don't touch me ! How could you think
of such a thing ?"

"I beg your pardon ! oh, I beg your pardon !
I forgot I was so black. What a fool I am !"
Frank had actually dropped on his knees, and
was making supplicating gestures with hands
ridiculously concealed in big white cotton gloves.
"Don't run away, Pansy ! please don't ! I
never see you alone, except just by chance like
this. Do listen to me ! You look so lovely—if
you only knew !"

"And you—you—you look *too funny !* "

Some imp of mischief so tickled Frank's
divinity at this moment that her voice rose

birdlike up to a high note, and she laughed from that giddy point till her slim body ached.

Oh, it was the most comical sight she had ever beheld, to see that nigger minstrel down there on his knees, with his black face grimacing in the moonlight. As Pansy drew a long breath when her laughter ceased, there came a gurgling sound in response that quickly changed the after-taste of mirth into dismay. Why, goodness ! Frank was actually sobbing. Large tears were trickling down his cheeks, leaving white water-courses.

"I love you so. I love you ; and you are only laughing at me," he indistinctly repeated, in a tone of tragic despair.

" Oh, get up, *please !* and don't talk rubbish," cried Pansy at that, stamping her little foot on the grass with impatience. " Go and wash your face, and dress like a Christian again, and do put all this nonsense out of your head ! "

She was so angry for her sister's sake, that she would have liked to beat her wooer as he knelt there—big, good-hearted stupid that he was. If only it were Rose now that stood in her place !

At that moment Mary Dawson's voice could be heard calling from the end of the garden, wanting to know where Pansy was—warning her the dew was falling.

Frank bolted up the wall with a nimbleness showing that his toes had found acquaintance before this with certain holes in the bricks and the strongest boughs of the pear trees; and Pansy composed her face to its usual wide-eyed look of sweet innocence, and walked obediently towards her guardian through the dusk.

When the London season is in full swing, some faint hum from its pleasure-seeking hive echoes even into the most sequestered country haunts. And so it came to pass that stout Mrs. Vyner, the rector's placid wife, and Mary Dawson, one of her best friends and gossips—only this last, be it understood, as regarded the villagers' hearths and the school forms, for human nature must have its safety-valves—these two least gadding of women mutually confessed a very strong wish to see a certain Exhibition in town, of which the rumours had stirred their minds beyond the

most popular reciter's latest comic sketch or
even the Academy and such-like sedate, instruc-
tive joys.

Frank heard of this weakness, and was
delighted. Why, of course, they must go!
They would all make a little party, and bring
Miss Rose Dean and—her sister. He put it
diplomatically to the others that the younger
sister ought to come; it was an education in
itself to see the products of other countries.

But to the surprise of not only himself, but of
the remaining listeners three, Pansy interrupted
her advocate with a quick refusal. She could
not be persuaded to change her mind, although
she would give no distinct reason for preferring
to stay at home. Inwardly she was verily
trembling lest she might be desired to go by
Aunt Mary; again in love's fever the sudden
wild hope of spending a whole long day alone
with her lover Craigdarrock made her heart
burn within her with a flaming fire she could
hardly hide.

Frank, who was more deeply wounded than
he cared to show, tracked his unkind nymph
cautiously all round the rectory orchid-house,

of which the warm fragrant atmosphere was
Pansy's delight.

Snatching at a minute's chance of being alone,
he reproachfully began—

" So you will not come to-morrow ! I thought
you might have cared to please me for once,
when you know *I* am getting up the party."

" I care to please every one, but this time I am
staying to please myself," was the indifferent
answer, given with a mischievous subtle smile.

In her secret rejoicing Pansy did not heed
the warning quiver in Frank's voice.   She
was drawing down and admiring the curious,
gorgeous blossoms, not even seeing the fawning,
doglike look in her neighbour's eyes.   In truth,
she was weary of his repeated hints and
reproaches, which, after all, meant to her mind
just next to nothing.   She did not guess that
Frank Vyner would gladly have kissed the dust
off her pretty, pointed shoes at that moment.
Alas, poor fellow ! he was desperately " hard hit."
It was not her fault that he so adored those
starry eyes which looked out on the world with
a sort of babyish astonishment as at something
new and wonderful ; her low voice and graceful

motions, which, though he was not easily susceptible to woman's influence, he knew with an
inward groan would never leave his memory,
even on the other side of the world, and years
hence.

Frank still tried to plead and urge a losing
cause.

"I hoped—I somehow fancied—— Would
you not care to give me pleasure by just doing
so little?"

Pansy slightly recoiled, imagining the widespread chestnut branches, thinking of the great
flags in the backwater of the shade of the
hazel copse. Frank, watching intently, perceived
a vexed look pass over her face like a shadow
over new-sprung wheat; her gaze appeared
vacant, as if the spirit within her had gone out
a-roaming. Although guessing it was useless,
he still went on desperately—

"Do you not like me a little—just a little?"

"Oh yes. I always did like you from the
first very well."

"But do you not like me better now? Pansy,
my——" Frank broke off, choked.

"No, I do not; only just the same," answered

Pansy, with sweet mercilessness. "Rose likes you best."

Frank turned in the narrow hothouse passage. A mist came before his eyes. He felt as if a bullet had whizzed, without warning, straight into his palpitating heart.

Next minute he braced himself, threw back his head, and walked into the cooler summer air without, resolved that none should mark aught amiss. But that leaden weight would lie heavy, if hidden deep, within him henceforth for many a day.

CHAPTER XV.

" The blossom had opened on every bough;
    O joy for the promise of May, of May !
    O joy for the promise of May !

.   .   .   .   .   .

" And a salt wind burnt the blossoming trees ;
    O grief for the promise of May, of May !
    O grief for the promise of May ! "

NEXT morning Frank Vyner and his mother
called with a fly to escort the Willow Lea
pleasure-seekers to town.

Rose was smiling, conscious of looking her
best in her prettiest gown, and secretly grateful
(oh, dear Pansy would not think it unkind !)
that her sister had chosen to stay at home.

What a mysterious perversity of mind in
Pansy, not to be delighted at the idea of so rare
a pleasure as a whole day in London—going to
the Exhibition, lunching, sight-seeing, in Frank's
company ! He was such a good host; knew

how to take such excellent care of ladies.
Auntie, too, was pruning and pluming herself
like a plump pigeon in her grey-blue silk gown,
with bonnet and parasol to match.

Pansy looked almost enviously at the rest as
the carriage left the gate, and they waved their
hands; for, after all, a whole day in London
was an unusual excitement. Sometimes auntie
had taken her charges up to see the picture-
galleries, but never without express permission,
for mammie seemed always nervous about it,
lest some accident should happen to them by
train or in a cab. And then she was always
too full of her own business ever to go with
her daughters, which would have been the
chief charm of the outing. Even to-day,
although auntie had carefully written her all
their movements, it seemed doubtful whether
she could spare time to meet them.

While so thinking, Pansy was running, as if
she had wings to her feet, by the winding
shrubbery path towards the weir. Then on
into the open paddock, when her steps slackened
speed, and she went further lingeringly, with a
sudden access of coyness, pretending to look at

a foxglove in the hedge, to gather some oxeyes, because *he* might be watching her, although still unseen himself. Slowly though she came, with light dignity and grace, the child's soul felt projecting itself out of her body to meet her lover.

How could she keep Craigdarrock waiting? —miss one moment of bliss with him? Was there any one like him in the whole wide world? Had ever such an one been born through the centuries?—this man of men!

Alas! a willow bough lay flung on the grass inside the gate, almost broken in two, its jagged ends just hanging by a strip of bark. The signal meant that Craigdarrock could not come that day till perhaps late in the evening.

Sick with hope deferred, Pansy stood still awhile, her frail figure actually trembling. She pressed her hands to her bosom unconsciously, looked down at the willow twig, then away at the hazel wood, and on, on into space. Not coming! A whole long summer's day she must remain alone with her cruel disappointment.

The first bitterness past, came a second

thought slowly. "Better have gone with the others ; it would not have been consolation, but something to fill the void." Some seconds the young girl stood in hesitation, then with sudden impulse darted away, running once more. Quick, quick ! she might yet overtake them !

Into the house flew Pansy like a summer breeze—upstairs panting. She pulled out her prettiest hat, snatched a pair of fresh gloves from a drawer, hastily called out a few words to an astonished maid. Then she found herself downstairs—running, running by the short cut through the meadows to the station.

Oh, how slowly poor Pansy's feet seemed to obey their owner's eager spirit when the second field had been passed ! On, on, just to this wych elm first, then to that bush a little bigger than its fellows in the straggling fence. Now surely it was but a few yards' distance to the next gate ! So, cheering herself by fixing and passing many little imaginary milestones before the goal of the railway station, Pansy at last reached the dusty high-road, feeling strangely exhausted, her heart beating with great bumps like a steam-hammer over which she had no control.

No train was in sight down the curving iron tracks, which her blue eyes searched in an anxious glance. Red as a rose for once, and panting with breathlessness, she entered the pretty station, with its tiny garden on the opposite bank, glowing with sweet-williams and stocks.

Ill luck! The train was gone—ten minutes ago and more! But if Miss Dean would only wait a quarter of an hour, another would be coming up, said the good-humoured station-master, who knew the young lady by sight, and admired her handsome mother immensely, not only for the generous tips, but for the brilliant smile she bestowed on him most Saturdays.

What a long quarter of an hour it was, as Pansy sat on a bench in the shade, watching the shadow of the wall creeping ever nearer and nearer to her feet, till they were left in sunshine! Then she sprang up restlessly, vexed that the horrid, little, wooden shutter of the ticket-office remained closed so long. The train was certain to be arriving this very minute;

she would be late. Tapping with light fingers impatiently at the wicket, Pansy besought the clerk in so winning a voice of entreaty that he gave her a ticket one minute and a half too soon, much amused.

Luckily this whimsical passenger found half a sovereign and five shillings in her purse, though she had hardly given a thought to money when starting from the cottage, like a young swallow adventuring itself in flight for the first time. Both the Dean sisters were always amply supplied with pocket-money. Their mother said means kept young people from being mean.

"I remember being in such straits myself as a girl, that once I picked up with actual joy a shilling some one had dropped in the road. I ought by rights to have given it to the nearest beggar," Stella used to tell with vehement self-pity; adding that after her marriage she was obliged to teach herself to be sufficiently open-handed, just as other young housekeepers practise economy, and her shame at niggardliness had been worse than theirs after extravagance.

Pansy glanced doubtfully now at the few silver coins left in her hand, wondering whether she had enough to bring her home. No matter, she was certain to meet auntie. Otherwise it was a pity that she spent so much last week on buying a half-starved puppy from a tramp, at the latter's own price. She had coaxed the rescued waif to Willow Lea with difficulty, when, lo and behold! after a good dinner, the vagabond withdrew snarlingly from her further blandishments, and, tucking its tail between its legs, vanished at full speed down the road in anxious pursuit of its late tyrant, being seen no more.

The signals were up. The train was coming. With an excited sense of carrying out her adventure, Pansy's lips parted. She turned her head and met Craigdarrock.

The latter started, slightly surprised out of his usual self-control, amazed, and—could it possibly be?—annoyed.

" What freak is this, my dear child? " he murmured, in a remonstrating undertone. " What are you doing here? "

But the doubting faint frown on his face

cleared, as Pansy artlessly and eagerly explained.

" So I am going to follow them, don't you
see ! " she cried, delighted as a child with a
new idea.

" But you cannot go alone."

" Why not ? I am not a baby. I have
money, and I can ask my way."

Then seeing a strong disapproval, mingled
with amusement, on the face which she had
learned to study as an astrologer the signs of
the sky, the corners of the would-be traveller's
lips drooped, blank sadness overspread her face,
and her eyes seemed looking at a dead wall of
disappointment.

Suddenly a new idea struck this young
witch, and, turning, she implored in her most
irresistible voice—

" But you are going too ! There is a ticket
in your hand. *Then will you not take me ?*
Quick, quick ! Say, ' *Yes.*' Oh, you must—
you will ! I want so to see this Exhibition,
like the others. Do not leave me a whole long
day alone at the cottage. Oh, I must go !
indeed I must ! "

The train came out of a distant tunnel with a prolonged scream. Craigdarrock stood a moment with knitted, puzzled brow.

"Here it is coming," bemoaned Pansy, in an agony of expectancy.

The long, black snake of carriages was rushing quickly towards them, winding behind its snorting engine. Craigdarrock gave one look at that eloquent childish face, the eyes pathetic with longing, the quivering lips.

He was lost.

Then the guard shouted, "Take your seats!" And somehow Craigdarrock and Pansy found themselves—he hardly knew how it happened —in a carriage together.

Next minute they were gliding off. The well-known pastures, woods, and distant range of low hills receded from Pansy's vision, while she sat there happy and smiling, but silent after her past tension.

"How picturesque she is!" thought the man whose eyes were watching her with a new light dawning in them—a reckless, passionate, longing gleam. To have his little sweetheart safe from any chance of their being vexatiously

disturbed, all to himself, was delightful, if wrong
for her.

"It is her own doing. You did not urge
her," whispered the worse half of the double-
natured being he often felt himself to be.

"What does she know of the world's ways,
that the tongues of scandal will be let loose
after her fair name like a pack of hounds?"
more faintly urged his better self, but far more
faintly,—it had been down-trodden, so often
well-nigh killed, long ago.

There was another couple—to Craigdarrock's
experienced eye, a honeymoon pair—at the
further end of the carriage. These hardly
noticed the last comers; they were too taken
up with reflecting themselves in each other's
eyes, holding each other's hands in half-con-
cealed fashion; ashamed, yet shameless.

·Pansy had given them one swift glance, then
dropped her long eyelashes that swept her
cheeks in a dark fringe. Her upper lip curled
in delicate scorn, yet she was secretly stirred.
Two red spots burned on her face. She moved
uneasily, troubled for the first time to discom-
posure beneath Craigdarrock's gaze, which she

felt burning upon her. Then, to hide her
uneasiness, the child-girl tried to prattle gaily
with unconcern.

"You will take me first to the Exhibition,
will you not? Even if we do not meet the
others immediately, we can see a little of
it together, you and I!" and she laughed
nervously, yet with glee, not quite sure in
her own heart, now, how auntie would take
her prank. "How surprised they will be!"

"They will be more surprised than pleased
to see me," whispered Craigdarrock, bending
forward. His knee just touched hers by
accident, his breath fanned her cheek.

"Ah! I forgot." Pansy shrank gently from
him, afraid, she knew not why. "You are a
stranger to them. No one knows. Then I
must go alone. That is it." Her face fell.

"It is so large a place, you might wander
for hours and never see them. You will get
lost in the crowd. No, no; that will never do."

"Then what *shall* I do?" A wet mist rose
before Pansy's eyes, and her sweet mouth
quivered, so that Craigdarrock was inwardly
wishing to kiss it into happiness again.

"Leave it to me. We two can spend a happy day together, can we not? We will go and see whatever else you like — Madame Tussaud's, the Academy, the Tower, or the Monument." He was laughing like a boy, feeling ten, nay, twenty years younger. "Then, later on, you can take an earlier train home, and meet the others, as if nothing had happened. There will be no harm done."

"*As if nothing had happened! There will be no harm done!*" The words seemed re-echoed dully from the cavern of the man's own mind. His better self tried to rise; the worse grappled, battled, beat it down, reiterating, "What is the use of thinking beforehand? Let things take their course, as chance will have it, Kismet!"

Soon the atmosphere began to darken perceptibly. They were rushing through a region of grimy houses, with backs turned to the line, past sooty brick walls, huge boards covered with flaring posters. Now into a great station darker still, filled with a strange, choking atmosphere, new to Pansy's lungs.

"A fog, by all that's unholy! A pea-soup

fog on such a lovely summer's day! London
has outdone itself!" muttered Craigdarrock
under his moustache. Then louder, "Now, how
shall I amuse you, pet?"

"We might go to a pastrycook's first, perhaps," murmured Pansy, shyly, with enticing
visions of ice-cream and sweet cakes tempting
her. "No, I am not really hungry, but a little
greedy, you know."

This in laughing reply to his eager inquiries and lover's solicitude lest she felt faint.

Why, she must be famished!

As they got into a hansom, Pansy felt half
stifled, yet hardly disappointed. It was so
queer, quite a funny experience.

"How dreadful!" she murmured, half laughing, with smarting eyes and aching throat,
looking up at the pall of sooty yellow vapour
that obscured the glorious blue sky.

Small heart had she for the Exhibition now.
Faugh! How could the fountains glisten, how
could the bands play, and the balloon go up in
such Egyptian darkness? She envied Rose no
more.

But for herself— *Craigdarrock was here.* They

two seemed driving unseen, almost unseeing, through the wondrous obscurity; while shadowy omnibuses passed like huge ghosts, hoarse voices shouted to each other from lighter vehicles, timid pedestrians were seen a moment, then lapsed into gloom. Through it all this naughty stray fawn felt as if bound to an earthly Paradise. Blessed fog! Welcome ten thousand such, so long as she was by her lover's side! Pansy could hardly believe her senses. The happiest, wildest day-dream of old was realized. He and she were out in the world together, hand-in-hand.

On, on through many and wider, therefore dimmer streets. Twice Craigdarrock gave orders to the driver. Twice he changed his mind, gnawing his moustache in perplexity.

"Those restaurants are both too crowded," he explained briefly, in answer to Pansy's inquiries. "I don't want you to be seen with me, and have acquaintances wondering who you are."

"No?" said Pansy, obediently, though mystified.

Suddenly Craigdarrock took a resolution on

impulse, and called out the third time. "The fog is so dark; it matters less," he said aloud.

Presently the hansom stopped. Craigdarrock helped his companion out, took her up a broad, gilded staircase, where their feet sank in thick carpets. Groups of gaslights and handsome chandeliers were burning as they passed down a spacious corridor as thickly carpeted as the stairs. Then came a room, empty save for their two selves, with bright lights burning, the blinds drawn to shut out the remembrance of the fog outside; an elderly fat waiter bowing obsequiously, a small table ready spread with delicacies.

Pansy felt bewildered till now by the strangeness of it all—the roar and traffic of the streets, the flare of the lights, and the daylight-darkness. But now she revived, utterly happy to be with the man she loved, feeling in shelter once more.

"You must drink my health," said Craigdarrock, with shining eyes; and he poured out a glass of champagne, which shone like liquid, frothing gold. "See, I drink yours, my dear little willow maiden."

" I drink to your happiness too," smiled
Pansy, divinely, raising the glass to her
lips.

" Ah ! " breathed Craigdarrock.

CHAPTER XVI.

"Un jour de fête,
  Un jour de deuil,
 La vie est faite
  En un clin d'œil."

"PANSY! Pansy! Little love, how I adore you! How I love you with all my soul and being! If you knew how hard I have fought to keep the mastery over myself! But there! —you have conquered, my blue-eyed queen. I am not my own master henceforth, but your slave, little one, darling."

Craigdarrock was standing under the gaslight, in order to see Pansy's face the better that strove to hide itself on his shoulder. The man was babbling in a happiness that flooded all his being and transfigured his face. He felt at last—at last—that this guileless child's loving heart was the pearl of price which

hopelessly he had sought as his ideal since
boyhood. Mysterious promptings of mind of
late had warned him this might be she; honour
urged him to flee.

This very morning, until meeting Pansy by
chance, vague suggestions had flitted through
his brain that, once in London, it might
be well never to return to the riverside—
nevermore.

And, see! Fate seemed to have decided
otherwise, against his will at the time; yes,
Fate had cast the die.

"Do you really love me better than any one
else ever before?" murmured Pansy, in his ear.

"Yes. I swear it on my word of honour.
More than that, I never have really loved till
now but once when I was quite young. Fifteen
years ago, sweet—think of that!—about the time
you were born. And I love you a thousand
times better, for that woman was false, while
you——! Oh, my little angel, you are true to
me with all your soul. You trust me, and you
shall not repent it. We must never part;
never, Pansy, do you understand?"

"Yes; I am yours till death."

The slim form the man held in his arms seemed ready to dissolve like a snow-wreath, faint with the exquisite vision of happiness his words had conjured up. Craigdarrock for years back had never or seldom tried to restrain his impulses; now he hastily formed a resolve.

"Listen, my pet! We will go away together this very evening to such a heavenly place by the sea. You love the sea. There will just be time to catch a train——"

"But I *must* go home first! How could I leave without telling mother? They would be so frightened! They might think me lost!" pleaded Pansy, her childish face paling suddenly at the enormity of such misconduct as he proposed.

Craigdarrock's smile of beatitude faded. "Come," he gently urged, "come to my home —our home! Trust me to put your dear heart at rest."

He gently drew her to the door. As they stood on the threshold, two other figures came out of a general dining-room at the end of the corridor. The one was a tall, slight woman, very fashionably dressed, who was accompanied by a grey-haired, stout man of aristocratic appearance.

"Wait a moment, dear! Come back!" whispered Craigdarrock, who recognized the approaching pair, and wished with sudden anxiety to shield his sweet companion from their cynical observation.

But, to his amazement, Pansy uttered a gasping cry, and stood transfixed. The young creature felt afraid—for the first time in her happy life. She stretched out her hands with timidity yet loving joy struggling together in her pleading face.

" Oh, darling, I have found you! *Don't be angry!* but I followed the others up to town, it was so lovely. By chance this morning I met my friend—you remember! Indeed, it is quite a wonderful story! and he brought me——"

" *You here, child!* God in Heaven! who has dared——?" screamed Stella, though almost inarticulately.

She had sprung forward, gripping the girl's wrists violently, her voice sticking between spasms that caught her throat; her lips, nostrils, even the surface of her cheeks, quivering in frenzied passion.

Horror-struck, her blood verily curdling at sight of such rage as she had never dreamed of, and that displayed by this beloved being, towards her own self, Pansy turned deadly pale, and trembled violently, speechless.

Even as Mrs. Morice broke off short with rolling eyeballs, her inflamed gaze fell upon Craigdarrock, who stepped forward.

"What! . . . It is you, Gordon Muir?—*you*, who once loved me! Ha! Is this your revenge?" she uttered with convulsed features, pushing Pansy aside, the words seeming to escape from her swelled lips only at the widened corners of her mouth. It was a terrible sight to see such human fury.

Only the intervention and soothing expostulations of the gentleman accompanying her, who thrust himself bodily between them, apparently stopped the agonized woman from attacking Gordon Muir. For by her clenched teeth and convulsively twitching fingers, she was evidently lost to all sense of self-restraint.

"Don't! don't! Oh, what is wrong?" pleaded

Pansy, at last uncovering her trembling hands from a miserably white face. "His name is Craigdarrock. You remember—I told you of him. He says we are betrothed. He loves me, indeed; and I—— " The young girl faltered, crimsoned.

" ' Craigdarrock ! ' I remember now; that is the name of your Scotch estate," hissed Stella, alternately knitting her forehead and furrowing it with a dreadful air. "So, Gordon Muir, you have deceived an innocent child by false promises !—*you, a married man !* "

A hoarse, faint cry came from between Pansy's blanched lips. But it was such a mute inward cry, the others hardly noticed it—did not know it was the wail of her spirit of childhood, with its happy innocence of evil, departing for ever.

"Leave me to explain my own affairs, madam," returned Muir, furiously. "What right have you to interfere, of all women alive? —you, who since last I had the honour of meeting Lord Middlesex in your drawing-room, fourteen years ago, have been the ruin of how many young fellows' lives, as then you

were of mine? What is this young lady to
you?"

"She is my daughter."

Both men could be heard drawing deep
breaths in the silence that followed. Then
Middlesex asked, in a whisper meant for Stella's
ear alone, that was careless of the eager anxiety
and pain in his voice—

"Which one?"

At that moment Pansy's slight figure
swayed. She dropped forward on her knees
before her mother, clasped her thin long arms
round the latter, and cried in accents of sup-
plication, that cut them all three to their hearts,
for never had any one of them heard so piercing
a note of agony—

"Oh, mammie! mammie! mammie! *I loved
him so! I believed in him!* Take me home!"

Next instant she sank in a white, senseless
heap on the floor. Middlesex lifted and carried
her back like a feather-weight into the room
which she and Craigdarrock had so lately
quitted.

Strange that Pansy did not recover consciousness, try what remedies they might to rouse her from that trance-like stupor !

A doctor was summoned in haste. There had been a severe shock to the brain, he gravely reported. The best, indeed the only chance, was to take the girl home at once, to let her feel herself surrounded by familiar objects.

On leaving the stricken mother, the doctor whispered more to Lord Middlesex, who way-laid him in the corridor, while Muir of Craig-darrock (for this, as chief of his clan, was his proper title) stood a few steps away, staring in gloomy stupefaction out of the window. He was not thinking; he was simply dazed by the late revelation. The thought uppermost in his bewildered mind was the memory of a baby playing at its mother's feet, and sucking a gold-topped smelling-bottle set with diamonds.

Was that the doctor speaking?

"If she recovers, she will most likely be an idiot for life. In any case, she is subject to heart-attacks that might be fatal any moment. The girl has the frailest organization I have almost ever seen."

The words were whispered pityingly, and

they made Gordon's blood run cold. Presently he was aware that Middlesex was speaking to him. They were alone together. The two men dared not raise their eyes to look at each other, as, with a heavy expression on both faces, they consulted in hushed tones.

"This is very painful, Craigdarrock; but you will have to go through it, so far as I can see, I am afraid, and see them back, lest worse happens. The poor girl is still more or less insensible. If there is not a great change for the better before night, *then*——"

The other shuddered.

"I will go," he managed to answer, with lips parched as dry as bones. "*Then—then—then!*" The word drummed in his ears like a repeated knell of dreadful despair.

"'I dare not go myself," confided Middlesex, trying to hide a tinge of relief in his voice. "Would to Heaven I could! But my wife expects me to start with her for Paris this afternoon. We sleep at Calais."

"Lady Maud and I are pretty well separated. I might have married Pansy, if only——" Muir's voice dropped in weary bitterness. (He could not utter the thought in his mind: "If only I had divorced my wife. And I might have done so but for the feeling that few men have the right to cast stones at a woman—certainly not myself!")

Middlesex rejoined the miserable mother, and, using all the influence he still possessed over Mrs. Morice, urged her to accept this arrangement of his, as she was not fit to judge for herself what was best.

"That villain go with us! Never, never! Let him not dare to cross my path again!" she cried, firing up once more.

"Be reasonable, Stella!" remonstrated Middlesex, in the tone of a compassionate judge condescending to argue with some unfortunate being distracted by grief. "You know well enough neither of us has a right to blame him. He only knew her by the name of Dean, and has assured me, on his sacred word of honour, that he never dreamed she was related to you. No man could be more bitterly sorry than he is."

"Tell him to nurse his sorrow out of my sight, then. Leave me to take care of my own child myself."

"I shall not do so. It is my duty to speak in this matter. Some one must go to see after you both. She might—— " Middlesex broke off, shocked; he had almost said, "die on the way."

Perhaps Mrs. Morice guessed as much, for her head drooped on her chest, while her features seemed to sink. An air of prostration had succeeded her last ebullition. She muttered, after a few moments' thought, with intense bitterness—

"Yes; let him come. Let him see out his own work to the end. It will be the most bitter punishment a man like him could have; and if she dies, he shall be standing by. Oh, I will not spare my sensitive fine gentleman any pang, not a single torture of mind that I can inflict. This shall haunt him to his dying day."

Then, rousing herself feebly with a sullen glow lighting her miserable eyes—

"And you, my lord, *how do you feel?* You first made me forget my duty to my husband, and grew tired of me, as you tired soon afterwards of your young wife. Cold-blooded and

selfish as you are, it was habit or passion, not
love, that survived, and brought you back at
times to see me. And I, out of my great love,
that turned to bitter gall, tried to tempt and
draw you again, that your wife might feel some
anguish too, and possibly think me a rival still,
however old and faded I had grown. Gordon
Muir, at least, may *feel*, though he is cruel. I
know still how to turn a dagger in his
heart! But you——! Heavens! that I had the
power to make you suffer, even ever so little, in
mind! Oh, you men! you men!"

"Women are so unforgiving, so ridiculously sentimental, even when they get on in
years!" This was his lordship's reflection, with
a shrug of cool disgust, when he had silently
bowed and quitted Mrs. Morice—for the last
time on earth.

* * * * *

So before that afternoon, which was still
sunny outside London's foggy veil, had turned
to cool evening, they brought back the pros-
trate, almost unconscious form of a dying girl
to the pretty cottage by the river.

The gardener was still whetting his scythe

as he was finishing the mowing of the lawn he had begun that morning. The birds were chirping as usual in the bushes; white tobacco flowers were beginning to unfold their night-loving blossoms. The hoarse noise of the weir sounded ceaselessly through the fringe of willows.

What was changed at Willow Lea? Naught —but that a lily hung half broken on its stalk,

CHAPTER XVII.

TWILIGHT came creeping on with hushed foot-steps and ever-darkening veil.

In the cottage drawing-room Mrs. Morice and Gordon Muir sat facing each other, listening intently, with pale faces and straining ears, for the door stood open. Upstairs, in her own pretty blue room, lay Pansy, white as her pillows. Rose was kneeling by the foot of her sister's bed, unable to remove her eyes from the motionless form that was again dearest of all on earth to her; that had always been best beloved, save for what now seemed a passing foolish fancy of the last few weeks. Mary Dawson was softly endeavouring now and again to revive the young life that she yet feared was fast ebbing away.

There was a hospital nurse in the room, just arrived from London. She soon confided to

Miss Dawson there was nothing to do but to wait. A great London doctor had come and gone.

Pansy's eyes were open, though turning so much upwards she hardly seemed able to notice what was going on around. Yet, while her mother was bending over her, she kept up a feeble moaning, which so went to Stella's heart that the latter crept downstairs, unable to bear it. Then the dying girl grew quieter, seemed to recognize Mary's touch pleasurably. Without doubt she had feebly smiled at Rose.

These two happened to have returned early from London, where the little pleasure-party was quite dispirited by the fog; also because Rose, while they were at lunch in the Exhibition, was seized with a strange shivering fit, that gave her companions some uneasiness. They believed she was really ill, she looked so pale and distressed.

"It is nothing," she however whispered to Mary Dawson, being ashamed of herself. "I only feel—I don't know why—as if something dreadful had happened."

So Mary and Mrs. Vyner, sensibly thinking

the girl had taken a chill in the fog, agreed to come home by the next train.

Muir, in his great misery, would have given half of his possessions to be alone, if only a while, his agony of grief and apprehension making it exquisite torture to remain in the presence of Mrs. Morice. But Stella guessed as much, and would not let her victim go. Once he did spring to his feet, on an impulse that he could not bear it, but her reproaches burst out with such contempt that, stung to the quick, he quietly sat down again. It was his punishment—he *must* bear it.

Craigdarrock's heart could hardly be quite hardened, for, in spite of his own despair, he found himself pitying the unhappy woman, who was suffering the worst throes of maternal anguish. Now she was wailing, muttering half aloud to herself.

Would she never stop? *If only she would be silent!*

"Oh, my child! my child! O God, my child!"

So the wretched mother repeated mechanically over and over again. At times came other sentences. These, if their sense reached Craigdarrock's brain, who held his bursting head between his hands, he sometimes answered almost unconsciously. His voice was so muffled that it was inaudible. Only at times, when his companion's passionate upbraidings vehemently demanded a reply, he forced himself to intelligible speech.

"Oh, my Pansy! my darling!" went on the one mourner. "I meant her to be so happy. Goodness seemed to me happiness, and she was reared in such perfect innocence of all evil——"

"Yes, and ignorance," mutely groaned the other mourner, in his tormented mind. "If your white dove had known the fear of danger, as she felt instinctively the promptings of her loving little heart, it might——! Oh, wretch! How dare I excuse myself? Was it not my duty as a man to have shielded her all the more from my own selfishness? Why did I not tell her outright I was not free? Coward! Villain!"

"All over now! Oh, my Pansy! my Pansy! The sweetest thing, I used to think, that ever God made. Every motion was grace. Then

the turn of her head; that long, curved neck;
her eyes———"

Gordon clenched his hands harder. His rack
of torture had been given an extra screw.

"Yes, I had laid by a good fortune for her,
so that she might choose as she pleased, and
make a happy match. Ah! my pansy is not
a heart's-ease now, but a branch of sorrowful
cypress! What man will ever wear it next
his heart?"

Gordon was choking. He opened his mouth,
but, though his lips moved convulsively, the
cry was only uttered in silence—

" What other man? She is my flower, nearest
my heart now and for eternity! She has sworn
it to me. We were destined for each other.
Naught shall part our two souls, now, henceforth, and for ever! If even we never see
each other more with bodily eyes, once across
the border of existence she is mine, and I am
hers."

" Why do you sit silent there, muttering
and making faces to yourself? You thief—you
murderer! You have murdered my girl, I tell
you! Her guilelessness, her joyousness in life,

are as dead as if you had killed her outright! Do you understand? Why don't you speak, man?" Stella's voice rose to a suppressed scream.

"Is it worse to murder a girl, as you put it, than a young man just beginning his life?" asked Gordon, hoarsely, stung to an audible retort. Yet he spoke without bitterness or anger any more, only in hopeless wretchedness. "You murdered me! When you first met me, what beautiful beliefs I cherished, that are all gone like morning dew! How I reverenced womanhood, and believed you the ideal woman, true, loving, only just not too good for earth! You called me your friend, melted my heart by confiding your—sorrows. To me you were sacred. Although I loved you with all a boy's ardour, I would have died rather than smirch your fair name. And then——! . . .

"I believed in myself, too! What dreams I had of being a good man! a distinguished helper of my fellow-men!—of hard work and the reward of feeling at the end one's duty well done! All over! You blasted my life, my love. All my noble ambition died. My faith in God, belief in woman, seemed extinct. They have revived—with love! but, God help me! they only make me feel the most unhappy man alive."

Stella gazed at him, miserable-eyed. She heard all he said, yet she was listening—listening for any sound of warning from the room overhead. Muir went on with the same hopeless calm; in such a tone one might imagine the dead addressing each other.

"If you had not so fooled me, I must have pitied you when Middlesex married; for you really loved him, I suppose. But after-wards——! *What* made you lead your terrible life? That I could never understand."

"The 'seven other evil spirits.' Passion and revenge on mankind and women, too, who had looked down on me," answered Stella from between her teeth. Then after a pause, she resumed, "All the good left in me has been my love for my children. And they adored me so. If you had not said to-day what you did, Pansy would never have known anything against me; she thought me so perfect! Oh, —you devil!"

"Hush, poor soul! Recriminations are useless between us. She thought me flawless, too, till you shattered that illusion. Believe me or not, I struggled hard with myself to leave her, as honour bade me. This very morning——Spare me your sneers! Had we gone together, she never would have learned of my first marriage. Till death I should have been devoted to her, made her happy as ever man could woman."

"A fool's Paradise. You would have made yourself a bigamist, I suppose—you who still pose as such a pattern gentleman! Why, I have even heard you called a model of chivalry in your behaviour to your wife."

"I might have broken the laws of my country for Pansy's sake—not our secret customs," returned Craigdarrock, bitterly. "What kindness and outward respect I have shown my wife has not been from hypocrisy, but a sense of duty. She asked no more in our hollow mockery of marriage." Then rousing to a sudden agony-point of pleading, "Oh, you who pride yourself on having cast aside all prejudice, do you not *know* I would have been true to Pansy till death? *Why* should I have sinned any more against a Divine law than the patriarchs of old, who were blessed, or thousands of upright Mohammedan gentlemen?"

"You cannot command love for life. I believed in Lord Middlesex," said Stella, gloomily.

"But honour, good faith, would remain. Had we but chanced to be born in another age or climate——! Oh, what a jumble it all is! We seem mere bubbles on the ocean of life, hurting each other, breaking, despairing!"

Craigdarrock's voice sank in weary dreaminess, but Stella was no longer listening to him.

"Hush!" she irritably commanded, straining her ears as she bent in a listening attitude. "Were they speaking up there? Pansy may want me." And she crept on tiptoe to the foot of the stairs.

"After all, so long as motherhood is not dead, there is still a spark of divinity left in woman," thought Craigdarrock, as Mrs. Morice moved away. "Yet all animals share the instinct with ourselves. Can something of divinity pervade the whole of nature?"

He rose and went heavily outside on to the fresh-mown lawn, the smell of the cut grass rising to his nostrils. He must escape, for a few minutes at least, from Stella's torturing reproaches. "Murderer!" "a would-be bigamist!" she had cast in his teeth. And she spoke truly. Evil woman though he thought her, she had taught him a lesson—who was so proud of his honour. While law exists, universal or not, those who break it are sinning against the trust of their countrymen—or are patriots. Foul he felt, to the innermost heart of him, as he went down mechanically to the willows, and stood looking at the rushing, untiring stream at his feet.

After all, what had he done worse than others? How many other men—— ?

Oh, false excuse! He, wise in the world's wisdom, had concealed his position and name—acted with open eyes. Pansy was a romantic child—an Eve who knew naught of the tree of knowledge of good and evil, therefore in very truth a victim.

Craigdarrock felt as if polluting the grass underfoot. Here, under this very tree, he had met Pansy first, her white dress fluttering in the light breeze. How the wind played that day with the tiny curls escaping from her piled-up hair, when she had flung off her hat down there upon the path, and stood facing him—those eager, supplicating eyes asking the stranger to save her kitten!

The memory of that first meeting was too painful. He turned and walked quickly back towards the cottage.

Who knew? Pansy might recover yet. Oh, how gladly Muir would give all he owned on earth, and his life besides, to save her bright young life this moment! Ay, if prayers did indeed avail aught, if there exists verily a listening, watching Providence, the strong man felt he could pray night and day that her existence should be spared.

Alas! to what end?

To lose her sweet wits, that had been so fine, so delicate? To linger on as a gibbering, senseless creature. No; better death by far, and that quickly, whilst she was still unconscious, and could not recall that both the beings she had loved so passionately were false to honour.

At that moment a woman's scream rang through the open window of the room above.

They had called Stella quickly, the nurse's long-trained eye having seen signs of warning. But the mother entered too late. A minute before Pansy had stirred her hands weakly, then folded them on her bosom.

The gentle heart, which always beat so feebly during her brief life, had received a shock that day from which it had no strength to rally, so with a sigh like a tired child, she fell asleep.

*   *   *   *   *

Ten minutes later, Stella was alone in the chamber of death.

At first, whilst the others stood by awestruck, praying from the depths of their hearts, she flung herself down, hugging the soft little corpse in her arms, covering the dead face, neck, hands, with wild kisses. None dared utter a word of consolation till her frenzy seemed exhausted. Then the daughter still left, Mary the trusty friend, feeling broken-hearted at sight of her grief, blotting out theirs, implored the unhappy mother to turn to their loving arms.

Stella rose, rigid as a statue, her mood changed.

"Leave me!"

She said no more, but look and gesture drove them forth. They heard the one door lock behind them, then the other.

She was alone now. No one could see—could stop her. Her hand crept down to her pocket, where she had lately concealed something.

CHAPTER XVIII.

THE watchers in the next room waited for what seemed to them an interminable time. It was an hour or more. Then the aged nurse took it upon herself to persuade her mistress to come away—to leave the dear dead body in her reverent charge.

The doors were locked, but inside she could hear agonized moans as of one in bodily as well as mental pain. A balcony communicated with Rose's room, and by this the old woman entered. She found Mrs. Morice writhing on the floor. An empty phial lay at her side.

So the tragedy was over. Pansy was dead. And now Stella was lying, in her turn, upon the bed to which they had carried her. Many remedies to save her life had been already used —more would still be tried, although some of the bystanders knew in their hearts it was but useless torture. All was in vain.

With failing eyes Stella saw the after-glow of the sun burning rosy through the dark trees that summer night. How still Willow Lea Cottage was! how peaceful! A blackbird was whistling in the bushes. Eight o'clock struck from the church tower down in the village. Strange to die so, and have *no more chance*—did the Creed say, she had learned in childhood? To have ruined her own life, and with terrible revenge felt glad to ruin those of others! To have staked her last hopes of happiness on the young girl who lay dead under a white sheet in the opposite room—and to have lost!

No more chance! Was that true? Would the nothingness she hoped for follow, or more, worse, agonies of soul? Or could there be a fresh beginning made—if even a more unhappy one than the childhood she had thought so unfair, more harsh than that of most girls; putting all poorer sisters on a lower social scale than herself as out of the argument?

Once the wretched woman raised herself on her elbow with a shriek.

"I used to believe there was no God," she gasped; "but, Mary, Mary, now I feel there is

one, an awful Judge, and He has done—to me
—as I did to—others."

Mary tried to comfort her. " He is a Father,
and He knows what it is to lose a child. He
pities you."

Stella gave a dreadful laugh.

"Then why could He not save my pure
daughter? Why is she punished for me?
The mother's sins visited on the child. It is
unjust!"

" No, no," pleaded Mary Dawson, big tears
rolling down her cheeks. " It is the greatest
check on sin, that the guilty feel they do not
alone suffer—their evil deeds must also hurt
those they best love. It is a simple law of
nature, don't you see that? Do not think of
it now, dear ; only think Pansy is perhaps
already with her God, who loves her with a
divine love beyond even yours. She is happy,
our poor darling."

" Shall I meet her where I am going?"
Stella moaned. " I love her enough to hope
not. She would be too sorry for me. Are
you sure, quite sure, she has gone straight
to Paradise? Oh! what is the right creed,

Mary? Is there a Purgatory and Paradise, as the parable says? or just heaven for her, and hell-fire for ever for me? Would not Mercy allow me to pass into nothingness—to forget? *What is the truth?*" Her voice broke off in a sharp wail.

"Surely the one great truth is that God is good, and is love," sobbed Mary. "Think of that, dear. You are suffering now; but it cannot last for ever. No, I do not believe that."

"My hell began some years ago, and has been burning in me ever since," went on Mrs. Morice, her voice at agony pitch. I once told you something of the kind; but you did not understand me. What was I saying? I forget!" and she stared with wild eyes and distorted features at the woman who knelt beside her, crying bitterly but quietly. "Oh yes! you used to think me a good woman all these years. How queer the world is! How one can keep secrets, even from those who think they know us so well!"

With the human craving to ease a burdened soul by confession in the hour of weakness and anguish of remorse, Stella, on regaining consciousness, had gripped Mary's arm, bidding her come near and listen. The tale she told was so dreadful that Mary recoiled with horror, her soul sick to loathing.

The friend she so trusted and respected had for fourteen years led a double life. This woman, who was so strict with her own young daughters, had enriched herself by shameful means—by laying her nets for the souls of men and innocent maidens, trafficking with hearts and human feelings as relentlessly as Shylock claimed his pound of flesh.

Still she held Mary's arm with clenched fingers. "Listen! I meant to leave off my life up there! I intended to turn over a new leaf in two months! I swear it! There was money saved up for my Pansy. I wanted her to be rich—rich and happy, as I never have been, while Rose is her father's heiress."

And to Mary's mind rose the words, "Thou fool, this night thy soul shall be required of thee!" But she was silent as the wandering voice went on—

"Who says I used to tempt other women? They came to my house of their own accord

—women of title as well as others. Pharisees! How they used long ago to look at me from under their haughty eyelids, because I had been only a merchant's daughter! Ha! it was a bitter joy to know that some of these fine ladies were no better than myself! Once I went to a ball at Lord Middlesex's house, and was proud of being invited. I was wiser afterwards. Remember, Mary, I never told you lies about making money in the City. I had lucky speculations now and again. You keep your money with an easy conscience."

Presently Stella's voice died away fitfully; she sank more and more deeply into unconsciousness.

Then only the faithful watcher allowed poor Rose to come in and sit by her mother's bedside.

Unhappy Rose! Stunned with this double shock, blind with weeping, the good girl was yet praying ceaselessly—praying with all her might and soul and strength for this passing spirit of her mother; for that of her young sister, too, which she vaguely thought of as now journeying further and further from earthly ken on its far aerial flight. And who can say but what such earnest prayer from a guileless heart may have availed much?

Only once towards midnight the dying woman slightly roused herself. The numbness of nearing death had relieved her now from her late terrible pain. Feebly she murmured—

" Can I be forgiven ? "

Mary spoke words of hope and consolation in those dulled ears. Rose, little guessing what this appeal meant from one so upright and flawless in conduct as she supposed her mother, pressed her lips on the latter's forehead again and again in kisses watered with tears of filial grief and blessing. That unction of love seemed to soothe Stella's flickering restlessness. Her features smoothed themselves ; the fingers twitched more feebly, then were still.

She never spoke again, but lay breathing heavily.

The watchers inside the cottage, who were close to the dread presence of death, did not know that outside, on the dark lawn, a man was seated on a bench under the old thorn—a bent figure, with dark head bowed and bare, careless of the falling dew, faintly grateful for the night breeze.

A man with a fire of remorse burning in his brain, never to be quenched whilst his sins remained in him; a worm of repentance gnawing in his tortured heart, never more to cease whilst he lived. Or so it then seemed to Gordon Muir; not feeling able rightly to realize pity, ruth, or love in his long-dead heart. Only misery, and always hopeless misery.

And whether a new life might yet come to him, being born again of the Spirit, in his present earthly existence, or if in some future state worm and fire would perform their task as they unceasingly have done through countless generations of sinful men, and so deliver his soul from its stains of evil, we may not know.

Craigdarrock had sat there since nightfall, through long hours in his agony, while the stars slowly passed from the east towards the now darker western sky in glittering company. He was dazed with the one thought that ceaselessly repeated itself a million times in his brain. At times its monotony stupefied him. He seemed to doze, then he roused again, and the same maddening thought beat on and on, as if the machinery in his mind had escaped from control, and must grind everlastingly till his body was worn out.

"Dead! Pansy dead! dead! Pansy dead— my little love! dead!"

A second voice within him seemed uttering remonstrances against the cry of its fellow-voice.

"Impossible! that airy, exquisite young creature, who seemed like a dancing figure, like Spring incarnate, with a lapful of flowers; not dead—she! Why, she was a very flower herself, hidden from the world, whose fragrance and beauty hardly any other man's eyes had ever lit on. A wood anemone, withering when plucked!"

"*Dead! dead!*" the other voice pitilessly repeated. Oh, dreadful thought, that the coffin-lid would soon be screwed down over that sweet small face Gordon had so lately passionately kissed to faintest tinge of rose; those eyes, biggest and bluest he had ever seen, out of which the love-light always shone on him with tender glory! Over Pansy's dear small head, with its dusky crown of soft hair ending in tiny tendrils, the red earth would be flung in clods, piled upon it by spade and shovel! Merciful Heavens! it was hideous. *Dead this evening!* She that had run so lightly across the fields before noon! And he, some one said, had murdered her! What treachery to that innocent, childish heart, given to him with such implicit trust, such utter love! *Dead at seventeen!*

So one after another the hours passed by, and no human eyes saw the man sitting there. The dews and damps fell on him, little breezes blew around, stars rode overhead, and the creeping, flitting creatures of night grew less afraid of the motionless being.

Could Craigdarrock ever forget that one and only look of reproach Pansy had turned upon him?—her last look? It would haunt him to his dying day.

And yet Craigdarrock was utterly sure that his dead darling had already forgiven him. Of that fulness of love in her gentle spirit he felt

more certain than of his own soul's existence,
than of any eternity to come. It was the one
anchor left to the man's storm-tossed mind.
Could he be so utterly worthless, after all, if she
had so cared for him, his poor little love, whom
yet till now he had not rightly loved? All
pure honest love, he believed, till he met Pansy,
had been withered within his heart since Stella,
her mother, deceived him. Then the sap stirred
once more, and green shoots sprang from the
dry tree.

The man bowed his head lower—lower. The
brand of this summer night's agony would
be impressed deep upon Gordon's inner man
henceforth, would even mark his features. To
himself it seemed that its burning pain could
never lessen, because there was no possibility
left of reparation.

Patience! Gordon Muir. Like all of us when
suffering agony, you forget what healing time
will slowly bring—blessed time!

In years that are still hidden, and at moments
on dewy evenings which bring memories of a
cottage by the pleasant banks of old Thames,
where alders and willows droop over the weir,

a thought shall come to this man with recurring, strengthening frequency—a hope that perchance he may yet meet Pansy's airy figure and sweet, pale face in some spirit-land; that she loves him still, pities, prays for him. Thus he will love her as he never did or could on earth, purely, as, with childlike innocence of evil, unlike the women of his sinful, everyday world, she had loved him. And so, dreaming, he feels as might Dives in Hades, had Lazarus been sent across the gulf to cool, but with a finger dipped in water, the tongue of the once-envied rich man.

Slowly the dawning light seemed to steal shivering upward from the east, growing, widening.

Twice the thought recurred to Gordon's mind of a woman on whose finger he had once placed a ring. She never loved him, but only married him for his broad lands; he her for her pride of birth, and her father's power as a great minister. False vows! false wedded lives! And now she hated him—wished to be rid of him; was unfaithful, too, as he to her. Poor woman! He did not blame her more than

himself.   But this, too, was heavy on his
soul.

Then came the burst of dawn.   Up rose the
sun to the *reveillé* of birds hymning the glad
light ; dews sparkled in diamond-drops upon
grass-blades, boughs, flowers.

And two dead women lay behind the drawn
blinds up yonder in Willow Lea Cottage.

CHAPTER XIX.

THE END.

AND the years rolled on. Only two years—four and twenty months; but how many the days and lagging to a waiting heart!

Then came a September, when the sunshine was sweet over living heads and the graves of the dead. Yellow sunflowers stared all arow and apples hung in gold and crimson balls in the orchards.

Two years ago Frank Vyner had sailed to Australia without a wife. Then the rectory settled down again to its old round of cheerful monotony. Now his parents' hearts rejoiced, for he was coming home for the second time—their firstborn, who lived so far away over the seas.

Little was changed in Willow Lea Cottage, where Rose still nestled like a lonely chick

under Mary Dawson's motherly wing.   Perhaps
the latter and Mrs. Vyner kept up some mutual
understanding, for from his mother's letters
Frank knew fairly well most of even the small
details and incidents in the lives of the
remaining two inmates of Willow Lea.   He was
even not greatly surprised that Rose was still
unmarried, except with that humble wonder a
man may feel at woman's constancy to a grateful, if unworthy, object.

On the very evening of his arrival, Frank
Vyner took his way towards the churchyard,
looking only a trifle older, graver, and more sun-
burnt than his former merry, boyish self.   The
great square tower threw a long shadow over
the fresh-mown grassy mounds through which
he passed.   Just where it ended, half in shadow,
half in sunlight, a girlish figure was standing
beside a white cross, on which she had lately
laid a wreath of white and violet pansies.   It
was Rose.

The girl looked up with a world of greeting
in her comely, fresh face, as if she had long
awaited the man.   Silently they grasped each
other's hands, and Frank Vyner did not relax

his clasp. Silently they both looked down awhile at the little grave and its headstone, on which was simply inscribed—

"PANSY DEAN,
Died aged 17."

And then and there, with his very first words, Frank Vyner told Rose that he was come back across half the world to seek her for his wife, if she would have him.

"Pansy would have been glad of it," he added simply, guessing the answer that was coming.

For happiness shone in the tears trembling on Rose's down-drooping lashes, and peeped forth in the quivering, doubtful smile that came and went on her lips, as if she was afraid of her own exceeding joy.

So Rose said him "Yea," modestly, even with humility, according to her nature.

Perhaps, being but a woman, although a good one, she might feel some pangs now and again in future, because her dear husband had not always loved her best. But it is seldom otherwise with wedded men or women, and

the happiest are they who are glad and thank-
ful for the precious love they receive, and do
not grieve over the measure which sweetened
others' lives, or even appeared wasted. Surely
the quality of love, like mercy, " blesseth those
who give " even more than they who take.

As for Frank, he felt that Pansy's sister was
nearest on earth to her who had been dearest
to him, and even to be reminded of his lost
love by a trick of speech, a turn of the head,
memory, association, was much. Yet in time he
grew to give his wife, if a less ardent yet a more
trusting, fuller affection than his once passionate
desire for Pansy. Rose was his steady friend,
a true helpmate. He leant on her in doubt and
trials as he could not have done, he owned to
himself, on the fragile, winsome creature meant
only to live in sunshine, whom the first breath
of sorrow's winter, the only cruel blow in the
battle of life, had stricken down.

Frank Vyner never asked or learned the
details of Pansy's death. If he had a faint
inkling of trouble, he did not in his loyalty
wish to know more. As for Rose, she had
been simply told by her good guardian that her

sister died of a fatal attack of the heart-disease
from which Pansy always suffered. No doubt
troubled the clear glassy depths of her mind,
nor would whilst she lived.

Faithful Mary Dawson kept well the promise
she had given, when Rose and Pansy were
babies, to their mother. She still shielded
Pansy's dear memory from the faintest suspicion
of blame.

So when these two young people, Frank and
Rose, sailed away half round the world to their
new home in Australia, Mary Dawson said
good-bye to England, and went with them.
There she still lives, brisk and helpful till her
days of work are done. "Dear old Mary," she
is called by Rose's merry, romping children.

And she will help to rear these babes, and
fit them better to face the thorns and snares
and flower-hidden pitfalls of life than was the
fair, fragile girl, whose name they learn to lisp
reverently as that of their sweet "Aunt
Pansy."

THE END.

PRINTED BY WILLIAM CLOWES AND SONS, LIMITED, LONDON AND BECCLES.

TELEGRAMS:
ASSIDUOUS, LONDON.

15, CRAVEN STREET, STRAND,

LONDON, W.C.

1894.

A Catalogue

OF

NEW BOOKS

AND

NEW EDITIONS

Published by

BLISS,

SANDS,

AND **FOSTER.**

*To be obtained
of all booksellers,
and at all libraries;
or of the publishers,
post-free on remittance of the published price.*

FICTION.

New Library Novels.—

A LIFE AWRY.

"Clever . . . . skilfully worked out."—*Standard.*

"A novel full of thought, power, pathos, and beauty. . . . A novel of remarkable loftiness and beauty."—*Daily Chronicle.*

"A realistic novel. . . . One of the most beautiful pieces of prose we have read in fiction for a very long time." —*Morning Leader.*

"Talented . . . clever. . . . The book is a pleasure to see as well as to read."—*Vanity Fair.*

By PERCIVAL PICKERING. *In 3 Vols.*

Dr. GREY'S PATIENT.

"Mrs. Reaney writes pleasantly, and these volumes of hers are very readable."—*St. James's Gazette.*

Miss Willard says:—

"Far above the ordinary level of the three-volume novel . . . nothing less than a human document."

"Mrs. Reaney is certainly to be congratulated."—*Review of Reviews.*

By Mrs. G. S. REANEY. *In 3 Vols.*

IN AN ORCHARD.

By Mrs. MACQUOID. *In 2 Vols.*

Author of "Patty"; "The Red Glove," etc.

DUST BEFORE THE WIND.

ANONYMOUS. *In 2 Vols.*

FICTION—*continued.*

THE MODERN LIBRARY.

Cloth, Gilt Top, 2s.
"Autumn Leaf" Tinted Hand-made Paper, 1s. 6d.

———

"Charming pocket series."—*Globe.*

"Charming volumes."—*Maxwell Gray.*

"Its binding, size, paper, and all other adjuncts are charming."—*Athenæum.*

1.—A LATTER DAY ROMANCE.

By Mrs. MURRAY HICKSON.

"A very pleasant little story."—*Literary World.*

"Dramatic power and artistic finish. . . . The book is good literature. It possesses distinction of style, force of expression, and quickness of insight, and is thoroughly interesting."—*Speaker.*

2.—THE WORLD'S PLEASURES.

By CLARA SAVILE-CLARKE.

"Forcible and fearless, while never overstepping the bounds of delicacy and decorum."—*Daily Telegraph.*

"The book is cleverly written."—*Queen.*

3.—A NAUGHTY GIRL.

By J. ASHBY STERRY.

[Just Published.

4.—"HEAVENS!"

By ALOIS VOJTECH SMILOVSKY.

A Bohemian Novel, translated from the Czech by Professor MOUREK, of Prague University, and JANE MOUREK.

[Just Ready.

5.—A CONSUL'S PASSENGER.

By HARRY LANDER.

———

(AND OTHER VOLUMES IN PREPARATION).

FICTION—*continued*.

One Volume Novels.

INSCRUTABLE.
By ESME STUART. Cr. 8vo. 3s. 6d.

THE STORY OF MY DICTATORSHIP.
ANONYMOUS. Cr. 8vo. 3s. 6d.

VICTIMS.
By F. W. MAUDE. Cr. 8vo. 6s.

A MERCIFUL DIVORCE.
By F. W. MAUDE. New Edition. Cr. 8vo. Cloth extra. 2s.

MISCELLANEOUS.

TWO WORKS BY FRANCIS H. UNDERWOOD, LL.D.,
Formerly U. S. Consul at Glasgow, and now at Edinburgh.

JAMES RUSSELL LOWELL: a Monograph entitled, The Poet and the Man.—*By* FRANCIS H. UNDERWOOD, LL.D. Crown 8vo, olive buckram, gilt top, 4s. 6d.

"Interesting touches of reminiscence and appreciation of Lowell and his contemporaries."—*Times.*

QUABBIN: The Story of a Small Town, with Outlooks upon Puritan Life.—*By* FRANCIS H. UNDERWOOD, LL.D. Numerous Illustrations. Large cr. 8vo, gilt top. 7s. 6d.

OLIVER WENDELL HOLMES says, in a letter to the Author:—"Dipping into it I became interested, and the more I read the more I was pleased, and so read on until I had taken every chapter, every sentence, every word, and the three notes of the appendix—lapped them up as a kitten laps up a saucer of cream."
The *Athenæum* says:—"His story is exceedingly well written, and is extremely interesting. . . . He has written a most interesting book, in which there is not a superfluous page."

THE ART OF PLUCK.—*By* SCRIBLERUS REDIVIVUS (Edward Caswall). New Edition. Royal 16mo, cloth extra, gilt top. 2s. 6d.

"The famous old 'Art of Pluck,'"—*Saturday Review*, and vide *Times, Speaker, Athenæum, Daily Chronicle*, and the whole press.

SPIRITUALISM.

The Autobiography of the greatest Living Medium.

THE CLAIRVOYANCE OF BESSIE WILLIAMS (Mrs. Russell Davies). With Preface by FLORENCE MARRYAT. Crown 8vo, with Portrait. 6s.

TRAVEL.

A WINTER JAUNT TO NORWAY. With Accounts (from personal acquaintance) of Nansen, Ibsen, Björnson, Brandes, etc.—*By* Mrs. ALEC TWEEDIE, Author of "A Girl's Ride in Iceland," and "The Passion Play at Oberammergau." Fully Illustrated. Demy 8vo. 16s.

SOMERSETSHIRE: Highways, Byways, and Waterways. With about 150 Illustrations, and about 256 pages letterpress. — *By* CHARLES R. B. BARRETT, Author of "Essex: Highways, Byways, and Waterways."

The above work is issued in two forms—

(a) The ordinary edition in crown 4to, bound in cloth extra, with four copper-plate etchings, on Van Gelder paper. Price 21s.

(b) A large paper edition, limited to 65 copies, numbered and signed by the author. This edition is in demy 4to, printed on the finest plate paper, and contains six copper-plate etchings. The work is sent in sheets, together with a portfolio containing a complete set of India proofs of the whole of the Illustrations. Price £2 2s. each, post free.

ALSO,

ONE UNIQUE COPY comprising, in addition to No. 1 of the fine paper edition an extra portfolio containing the whole of the original drawings, mounted. Both the copy and the two portfolios will be elaborately bound by ZAEHNSDORF. Price Fifty Guineas

CHILDREN'S BOOKS.

NURSERY LYRICS.

By Mrs. RICHARD STRACHEY.

WITH ILLUSTRATED BY G. P. JACOMB HOOD.

Imperial 16mo.   Price 3s. 6d.

An alphabet designed by the artist is inserted in the volume so that the donor may cut out the child's initials and fix them in the spaces provided on the cover.

"Pretty quaint nursery rhymes. . . . Sweet and simple."—*St. James's Budget.*

"A funny little excellent book for children is this. . . . Will delight the small folks by day, and send them happily to bed at night."—*Black and White.*

"Will certainly haunt childish heads."—*Graphic.*

"Merry jingles."—*Times.*

THE ADVENTURES OF PRINCE ALMERO.

By WILHELMINA PICKERING.

ILLUSTRATED BY MARGARET HOOPER.

Second Edition.   Fcap. 4to.   Cloth Extra.   Price 3s. 6d.

Opinion of the Press on the First Edition.

"An original and charming tale of the fairies of the sea, told with much grace, and riveting our interest throughout. The Author, in her preface, makes modest apologies for appearing in print; but no apology, indeed, is needed, and we shall hope to see more of her work."—*Athenæum,* November 29th, 1890.

HERCULES AND THE MARIONETTES.

By R. MURRAY GILCHRIST.

Illustrated. Fcap. 4to. 3s. 6d.

CHILDREN'S BOOKS *(continued)*.

THE STORY BOOK SERIES.

Royal 16mo. Half-cloth extra, and Cupid paper. 2s. 6d. Illustrated.

1.—STELLA.

By Mrs. G. S. REANEY.

" Much taste and good sense."—*Spectator.*
" An admirable gift-book for girls."—*British Weekly.*
" A dainty little volume . . . a charmingly-written story."—*Glasgow Herald.*
" Simply and prettily written."—*Scotsman.*

2.—MY AUNT CONSTANTIA JANE.

By MARY E. HULLAH.

" Pretty little book."—*Lady's Pictorial.*
" Gracefully imagined . . . prettily told . . . dainty illustrations."—*Scotsman.*

3.—LITTLE GLORY'S MISSION,
AND
NOT ALONE IN THE WORLD.

By Mrs. G. S. REANEY.

4.—HANS AND HIS FRIEND.

By MARY E. HULLAH.

MR. RUSKIN *says :—*

" I have read Miss Hullah's story with very great pleasure to myself, and heartily think she has the power to take good position and make her living very happily. It is of course a little founded on Andersen and other people . . . . but she's very clever herself."